A Certain Strain

of

Peculiar

A Certain Strain
of
Peculiar

Gigi Amateau

CANDLEWICK PRESS

First edition 2009

Library of Congress Cataloging-in-Publication Data is available.

Library of Congress Catalog Card Number 2008935295

ISBN 978-0-7636-3009-6

2 4 6 8 10 9 7 5 3 1

Printed in the United States of America

This book was typeset in Berkeley Oldstyle.

Candlewick Press
99 Dover Street
Somerville, Massachusetts 02144

visit us at www.candlewick.com

This paper contains 30% recycled post-consumer fiber.

To my blue-eyed Grammy, for showing the way home

"Something hidden. Go and find it. Go and look behind the Ranges—
Something lost behind the Ranges. Lost and waiting for you. Go!"
—Rudyard Kipling, *The Explorer*

Chapter One

WHAT HAPPENS IN MY MIND SOMETIMES is complicated. I mean, the brain is the command center, right? Sometimes my brain can't even command me to breathe. First my nose completely bails on inhaling. Then it's like my mouth even forgets how to open up and take a breath. All respiration stops, and my brain really panics. If it worked right, my mind would slow down and remember: the nose, mouth, and lungs are waiting for the command, "Go."

Instead, my brain shouts, "I can't breathe!" The respiratory parts hear *can't,* so they don't. My mind thinks I must be dying. Some smallness in me is usually right there, whispering, *Calm down, open your mouth, breathe, calm down, open your mouth, breathe.* But the thought of dying takes over and grows so big, so fast, that my chest starts hurting, maybe from lack of oxygen. Then I think that I am having a heart attack. I am only thirteen. Whatever is happening to me, when it is happening to me, I am afraid to die.

Mom thinks what happens to me is a panic attack; I call it my fear of dying. I don't think that's really what it is, though. I think it's more a fear of never belonging.

I am looking at the back of Drew Walker's head. Even now, after everything, I want to touch the waves of his hair. There is not a girl who doesn't love him, who doesn't imagine being kissed by him, who doesn't rush to enter a doorway just in front of him. He likes to place his hand on the small of girls' backs as a protective gesture—except mine. Not once has he placed his hand on the small of my back. Well, he did once, but it wasn't for real.

For the fifth consecutive school day, I have kept a silent vigil. Now I also force myself deaf to the too-close-to-me sound of Drew telling his friends about a girl he met over the weekend. I hear where this conversation will end. I look for a way to really go deaf, just until I can get home. I pick up my hands, all casual, and put them under my hair, over my ears. Then my leg itches, and as hard as I try not to scratch it, I reach down just to touch the spot on my left calf that itches and I hear the rude boys again.

"Was she, like, hot at *all*?" one of them asks.

Drew laughs. "No, she was disgusting."

"Like a three?"

"Worse than a three," Drew answers.

Without lowering his voice, the worst of those boys asks, "Was she as bad as Mary Harold?"

I keep my silence and scratch my leg. Then I stop breathing; my chest pinches so tight that I feel sure I am having a heart attack this time. I wish I had my phone to text Mom to help me; the smallness is at least able to ask for help from Mom.

"I'm afraid of dying," I might manage to squeak out if Mom were here in person. Mom can always look at me and see how tense my neck is, how frightened my eyes are, how I am in a world of trouble.

The boys sit right in front of me, wondering right out loud if there could ever be a girl more disgusting than me. My face turns violet, I'm sure of it, because I fear that my skin will not hold in all of the blood rising up into my head. I seal myself completely inside my hair canopy, so no sound can get in and no sound can get out.

People shouldn't bind their hair to stupid promises. Even five-year-old people should know better, but my ex–best friend, Krystal, and I made a hair pact back in kindergarten. Back when we both had real short hair, back when we both said *I love you,* we vowed that as long as we were friends, we would never cut our hair. Krystal cut her hair a long time ago, even before she dropped me. My hair has kept growing.

I hide deep in the silence of my long black hair. Drew and his posse aren't talking about the gross weekend girl anymore. They are talking about me and my favorite sweater and ripping about how my mom must never do laundry.

I wear this navy pullover every day to cover my boobs because they're getting big. I'm the one who forgets to wash the sweater; I do our laundry since Mom works so hard. The stupid sweater is hand-wash only. I hate hand-washing; we have a crappy laundry room without a good place to let hand-wash stuff dry.

I fight my own urge to kick Drew's desk over and over until he shuts up. Instead, I sink way away. I imagine that I am not one of them; I am the blackboard, or the desk, but not the grossest girl.

"Miss Woods, please answer the question."

I am not the grossest girl; I am the pencil lying on the desk.

Every desk squeaks; I feel all of their heads turn to face me. I need air. I keep on staring at my college-rule paper, thinking maybe I can write myself between the blue lines.

"All right, Mary Harold, enough is enough. If you can't come to class prepared, don't bother showing up."

I vanish, again, into the black forest, where no light can get in. I wish I could block out these sounds; I crawl deeper, and still, I hear the desk drawer open. My teacher's pen rips across the demerit slip. She tears the demerit off its pad and flicks it up above her head. "Get out of my classroom."

All of them laugh; I leave. In the hall, I press my cheek against the cold cinder-block wall to jolt myself into a new pattern of breathing.

I duck past the office window and run into the library. The librarian notices me sneaking in but doesn't ask for my pass. She never asks. I give her my usual *thank-you* eyes and rush to find a corner where I can fall into the earth and never come out.

Chapter Two

THIS COULD BE HAPPENING to anybody. Maybe a girl gets caught picking her nose, and that day, at that moment in time, it's the worst thing to do. The next day a different girl might stand in the same corner of the same hall and dig even deeper—so deep she ought to get a license. Maybe even more people see her, yet nothing happens.

One boy might own a case of dandruff so intense that it's a significant meteorological event, but only his parents and his doctor know that it's a real disease kind of thing. Maybe until Thanksgiving nobody really notices because the kid is kind of quiet anyway and keeps to himself. But on the day that the loudmouth boy whose dad is on the school board notices—on that day—it's all over. After that, it doesn't matter that once you get to know him he's funny and smart and that in a week the dandruff will be gone forever.

That's how it was with me.

I didn't get it right away. I mean, I don't dig so deep that I gotta have a license; my major hygiene issues are under control. Sometimes I forget to brush my hair or my teeth, but only because I'm running late and because I'm having so much fun, or at least I was.

Back in the fourth grade, and for a long time before, soap, water, and perfect hair were like our enemies. We were all sort of rough and tumbling around outside in the dirt and grass. But one day, in just one day, everything changed.

I wish it hadn't.

Krystal moved to Virginia from Tennessee in kindergarten. She was named for the hamburger chain; it's my favorite place to stop in Knoxville on the way to Wren when we visit Ayma in Alabama. The burgers there are so tiny that I eat three, or sometimes four. Sometimes on our way to Wren I totally fast until we get to Exit 398 off of I-40 so that I'm good and hungry when we get there. Mom's the same way. Then we buy a whole sack and load up on itty-bitty cheeseburgers and just split one order of fries, because, well, you can get fries anywhere, really.

Every time we get close to Exit 398, I tell myself I'm going to try one of those tiny hot dogs all the way this time, but I never ever do because I cannot bring myself to break away from my favorite cheeseburgers on earth and you won't find them until you're almost out of Virginia.

Krystal didn't know anybody at all when she moved here, and I was the only one who had ever heard of burgers with a girl's name. I have evidence, in the form of photographs and a two-page letter with nineteen hearts and way too many exclamation points to count, that Krystal and I really were best friends; it's not my imagination. We truly loved each other and told each other so, often.

When I hang up the phone with someone I love, like Mom or Ayma, I pretty much always end the call by saying, "Love you." That was our friendship. When Krystal broke her arm, in the fourth grade, I wrote on her cast: *Get Well Fast, I Love You,* with hearts all over the place. She told me, "I love you, too." We were best friends. I mean, I was ten. I did love her.

Krystal got teased so badly about what I wrote; the boys said we must be funny together. Krystal outright dumped me. She didn't just float away from me toward the other girls like what sometimes happens with friends. She flipped from being my best friend to hating my guts overnight.

After that, everything changed because everything suddenly mattered. Even things I didn't understand. To people who used to like me, I became like a game. The thing is, though, I hadn't changed at all from one day to the next; I was the same girl. And since Easter break of the fourth grade, it's been like that. I will never understand.

Now, every time I eat my lunch, I get hit upside the head with a carton full of chocolate milk from somewhere I cannot see. The milk bomb comes from a different table every day. In the mornings and afternoons, I sit in the front seat of the bus to avoid being tripped up.

So I never got it that the black ribbons were about me, too.

I had been thinking about them. Everyone in my grade is wearing them now—simple, elegant black ribbons. Last Friday, I worked up the nerve to ask Krystal for one, she being the sole ribbon-giver. She curled her lip at me. "*You* want one of these?"

She pulled one out of her back pocket and dangled it in front of me. I mean, she was keeping them in her pocket like she was one of those balloon clowns at the Golden Coral on Thursday nights, when kids eat free.

"You're not like us; you're not one of us. Every time you see this ribbon, you know what it means? Everybody hates you. *Everybody*." That's what Krystal said when she handed me a black ribbon.

The black ribbons. Hating me. An official club. I took the ribbon. What could I say?

Don't hate me. Look at me—I'm the same. We're the same. I love you—don't you remember?

Don't you remember?

So that day, Monday, four days ago, I just stopped talking to anyone, because who cares? School is finished next week. I was finished long before. In some ways, with no one looking at me or speaking to me, this week has been easier than the rest. In one week, I have almost learned to disappear. I wish I had figured this out a long time ago. I also wish Mom and I had moved back to Wren a long time ago, or I wish we had never left.

CHAPTER THREE

I CANNOT IMAGINE LEAVING MOM; I cannot imagine staying here. In her heart, I think she understands why I have to leave. I am her child, and I got the way I am from her.

We were even born in the same town: Wren, Alabama. Mom had been gone for years by the time I was born, but moved back there just to have me so I would have roots and a sense of myself. I lived there for the first three months of my life, until Mom found a job in the Pocahontas Forest. I like the fact that although I have not done my growing up there, I still count as being from Wren. For my whole life, I have always imagined what it would be like to live in Alabama with Ayma.

Except for when I was a baby, we've only visited, though. Mom left Wren, and her own family, the day she graduated high school. She was outcast in Wren for specific reasons that she keeps to herself. I know Mom was a hell-raising girl in a tiny Alabama town, which to her means narrow-minded people can't fit alternative girls into their narrow little worlds. To some people, my being born out of wedlock, father unknown, is a sin. According to Mom, around Wren, that is a sin that will send a girl straight to hell.

I don't believe in hell; not in a hell that somebody can be sent to, anyway; not in a hell where the devil might be waiting to torch an unwed girl carrying a baby. I do believe we all get a little touch of hell when we get separated from the people we love, even our friends from kindergarten.

To me, hell is not a flaming, fiery furnace where everything you ever did wrong scorches you to a crisp. Hell's not about what you did that's bad. Nope, if your heart is right, God will forgive anything and everything in an instant whether people want to believe that or not. The Bible sorta says that and, more important to me, Ayma says that's so, and she would know because she knows God.

Nah, I figure, hell is cold, damp, and lonely—a

place so sorrowful that even the daylilies won't grow—and daylilies thrive on neglect. Ayma says that's so, too, and she would know because she knows daylilies.

Mom and I walk hand in hand down our Virginia street to Rattlesnake Creek. The wind has blown all of the clouds away, and I can even see a sprout of crescent moon against a sky that's quickly re-forming into a new storm. I love seeing the moon in the daytime and have missed it over the past few days. Seeing just a wisp of it, waxing toward full, gives me hope. I have brought Mom out here to talk about finding some hope for me.

I look around Rattlesnake Creek. The sky has turned that freaky, alien yellow-green that often pops up between big storms. When the air is this eerie color, I wish for a spaceship to scoop me up. I would be so cooperative and peaceful, and I'd ask nicely if we could cruise right up alongside the moon.

I take a shallow breath and then another. I wrap both arms around Mom and try to breathe steadily.

"I'm afraid of dying," I tell Mom. She kisses my cheek forever, and I know that she is trying to kiss some of herself into me because she does this all of the time. I breathe in her kiss and as much of Mom as I can, too.

What can I say that's any different?

Mom swallows hard and doesn't look at me; she

stares down at the creek, and we both watch it rising, almost to the bridge.

I make her nervous. She knows that I am like her.

Times like this, watching the creek with Mom, are like tiny islands of heaven. But tiny islands get washed away too easily. I need my grandmother, Ayma. I need the real Ayma, not Ayma of the heart and the memories. I need Ayma of the body and blood, Ayma of the cooking and cleaning; I need Ayma of the holding me tight. That Ayma, the real one, is six hundred ninety-one miles away in Alabama.

The thunder claps me back to Mom, and I know that I am asking Mom, now, for a change. Just this one time, she needs to side with me like she sides with her creek and her forest. I want her to see that I need to leave. I brought her into this storm to ask if we can move to Wren.

I take in the most air my lungs will hold, and then I breathe out slow. "I can't live here anymore. I feel like I am dying inside, every day. I need to go back to Wren to be near Ayma. Can we go home to her?"

I watch the muddy creek water rise; the creek's grasses are flattened out now and not slowing the runoff at all. The leaves on the oaks and poplars have flipped up and are just waiting for a new wind to whip them back over or tear whole limbs down completely.

"Cricket." Mom looks at me. Mom calling me Cricket, her special name for me, is her way of begging me to keep going along, acting like everything is fine. "Cricket, school's almost out. Can you wait and see how the summer goes? Why does it have to be now?"

I don't answer.

Instead of answering Mom's questions, I tuck myself under her armpit and look down at Rattlesnake Creek. I think I would almost like to ride the creek to the river to the spot where it empties out at the flat water. Where the river falls over the dam, I might even remember to breathe.

I look up at the sky, and I wait long enough to let Mom remember how outcast she felt and that there was nothing that could have made her stay in Wren.

I skip over the part where I should now tell Mom about the black ribbons. She would only fuss at me: "Why don't you ever defend yourself? No one else is going to stick up for you, Cricket."

If I tell her now that I'm the grossest girl, she will take my hands, both of them, and insist that no I am not gross; I am beautiful. She will ask me if I want her to kick Drew Walker's ass. Then she'll make a joke about that because deep down she'll remember that Drew Walker is a child and she'll feel bad about even joking about whipping his butt. But the joke won't be funny; it will make me cry.

Thinking of all of this now, I decide.

I rest my head on Mom, and she runs her hands through my hair. The rain has picked up; the thunder and lightning are only five seconds apart now. The storm is almost here. Mom doesn't pay the stubborn weather system any mind; she stands on the bridge holding on to me.

I think what bothers her most of all is my needing Wren—the place she left and where she has only ever returned as a visitor. I suppose I could run away, to Chicago or New York, but that is not my purpose. My purpose is not to run away at all. I want to go home; I want Mom to come with me; I want us to start a new life together.

Mom slips her arm into the crook of my elbow and leans into me. I am taller than she is now, but Mom doesn't seem to notice or mind. The rain is coming back strong now; we walk back up the hill, caught in violent downpour. The sky throws down an avalanche of rain, and we get caught. The ground is already so saturated that a deluge of runoff water from our neighbors' yards overtakes our ankles. I lock elbows with Mom, like I used to do with Krystal. Arm in arm with Mom, I fight my way home, uphill all the way.

Chapter Four

"WHAT ABOUT WREN?" I ask for the gazillionth time.

Mom's not listening to me. Private-school brochures and applications are sprawled across the dining-room table. She barely looks up.

"Can't we both move to Wren and live with Ayma? Maybe a job will come open in the Black Warrior Forest. You've always wanted to work there. The Black Warrior is your true-love forest, right? Your favorite tree on the planet is there, the original Big Tree!"

In Wren, there is a champion poplar tree deep in the Black Warrior Forest. I've never been there, but that one yellow poplar is Mom's first tree-love. That big tree is probably five hundred years old or more, but we won't know for sure until she comes down on her own due to disease or lightning or possibly an ice storm. There's not an official trail to the Big Tree, and there's no marker, either. You just have to know how to get there, or know somebody who knows. Mom calls the Big Tree Sophia.

Every time we go back to Wren, Mom spends an entire day walking to Sophia all by herself. One year she got there and found that people had carved their initials into Sophia. She went into a little depression that year the tree was desecrated. Mom cries every time she loses a big tree. She is sort of a crybaby about her forest.

"What about Wren?" I practically shout.

She looks up like she has only just now heard me. I listen to Mom explain that I can start over here. Knowing full well that we can't afford thirteen thousand, or even six thousand, dollars a year in private-school tuition, she tells me, "We'll figure it out." Even knowing that we've missed the admissions deadlines for next year, Mom's still dead sure that "with your grades, none of these deadlines matter."

Mom wants me here. She offers to sell the Prius she just bought and go back to driving her old pickup truck.

"Those little cars are appreciating every day," she

tells me. "Let's sell it and send you to private school. I knew I kept the truck for a reason. You can start over at a new school."

We did keep the truck for a reason. I shake my head fast. "You said the truck is mine. We're saving it for me, when I can finally get my license, right?"

I already know how to drive. Mom is totally old school when it comes to driving. She thinks a girl should learn to drive on a stick shift.

Check. I learned to drive on a stick.

She thinks that anybody, girl or boy, who can't drive by age of ten is an idiot.

Check. I was driving by nine, therefore by Mom's rule, I'm no idiot.

Mom might not ever be ready to run home to Ayma; I am ready.

I hold her face and beg for what I know will be the last time, "Couldn't we move to Wren?"

Then I wait for the Holy Spirit to do its work. That's what Mom calls it when you ask someone a hard question, then don't say anything. She says that after you ask an important question—one that you really, really need answered—you risk interfering with God's work if you get uncomfortable with the silence and start talking again or asking more questions. She taught me that you have to honor the silence and allow whatever needs to come forth to go on and come forth.

This silent vigil is different from the kind I've been keeping at school. If I did stay here with Krystal and Drew and the Black Ribbon Club, I would erase myself completely into that silence and might never come back out. I hope Mom will break this silence of the Holy Spirit by speaking, loud enough for my ears to hear, the relief that I need.

I need Mom to be my mom and to tell me that my life matters and that she will move with me to Wren. She needs to promise I will be all right, that I'm not the grossest girl, that someone somewhere, maybe in Wren, will find a reason to be my friend for life, and that Mom and I can start over, together. She has to get this: my life is not her life. I am different.

Mom begins to cry. I've gotten good at waiting for the Holy Spirit to work; it's harder when she's crying. I want to tell her to forget about it—we'll talk later. But I resist the urge to hold her hand. I put my head down so her big tears can hit the table without me having to see them. I wait.

Finally, Mom speaks into the silence and stumbles through her tears. "I am not going back to Wren. There is nothing and no one for me in Wren. I closed that chapter before you were born. I have no future there, only the past."

I keep my silence.

Mom reaches for my hand, but I pull it back from her. "Please don't leave me." She begs me.

I'm thinking the Holy Spirit needs more time; I am quiet.

Mom's shoulders jut up and down, like she doesn't know the answer I want, but she does know. She keeps shrugging repeatedly. She cries with great tremors now instead of tears. I want to curl up with her, but I need my own relief.

I have done everything to belong here. All of it made no difference because no matter how badly a person wants to belong, belonging can't be forced. I speak it aloud, this thing I need. I don't ask; I tell her one last time and hope she hears me not in her ears but deep in her heart, where this must be heard, because I will not stay and she must understand.

"Mom, let me go. Come with me or let me go to Ayma." I wait, again, but I won't wait forever.

CHAPTER FIVE

MY LEFT CALF ITCHES something fierce, and that would be Ayma calling to me. There is a big chocolate-colored oval mole right on the inside of my left calf. Ayma has a mole exactly like mine, in exactly the same spot. I call my mole my *Ayma spot*. When I'm far away from Ayma, my mole keeps me connected to her. My belly button keeps me connected to Mom, reminding me of her directly. Everybody has a belly button to connect them to their mothers, but who else has a chocolate Ayma spot?

Seeing as how I never had a father, I haven't missed

one. My ex-friend, Krystal, has one who is a big, fat jerk. Instead of being addicted to trees or something the way Mom is, he is addicted to Wild Turkey, and I don't mean the bird. Krystal's dad drank his Wild Turkey bourbon on the rocks. Probably everyone has some addiction or another to keep them free of their pain, for the most part. But I wouldn't want a father like that guy.

On the other hand, I do like thinking that somewhere on this planet my father might wonder about me or even know about me. Maybe he's quiet like I am. Could be that he likes history, like I do. We might have a few little things in common.

There's a piece of me that could be my place of belonging with him like my belly button is my place of belonging with Mom and like my mole is my place of belonging with Ayma. On my right foot, and only on my right foot, my second toe stretches up way on past all of my other toes, even on past my big toe. My left toes are all of normal length. I just have this ugly old, crooked old, long second right toe. Ayma doesn't have one; Mom doesn't have one. I just wonder.

I almost run upstairs and wake Mom up. "Mom," I would say, "please, really talk to me about this. Did you ever feel this way?"

Even if I said all of this about me belonging with Ayma *and* Mom and all of us belonging together, I still think Mom wouldn't change. So instead, I leave her a note:

Mom,

If I don't go, how will I ever know where I belong?
Please, Mom, stick with me. Please.

Love 4-ever,
Cricket

I prop the note on the coffee machine and walk out the back door at two o'clock in the morning. Wearing my Lucky Jeans, which Mom bought me half-off when I begged for them, a Hurricane Katrina benefit T-shirt that says HOPE because I need some, too, and an old gray hoodie for the drive, just in case I get cold, I shift the truck into neutral and ease down the drive without so much as snapping a twig. My mole rubs against my jeans, and I know that by noon tomorrow, I'll be with Ayma.

Even maybe if we're not aware of it, I bet that every single one of us has a beauty mole on their calf, or an ear tag, or a crooked pointer finger from a special ancestor.

I know all about genes; this is different. I think maybe we have special marks because special people are there to look out for us and to guide us. Maybe our special person gives us a sort of shield of protection.

Ayma is my special person, and I'm going directly to the source.

Chapter Six

SOME PEOPLE DON'T UNDERSTAND the deal with kids driving young. Country people understand. There was a big story last fall about a kid—he was like nine or ten—stealing a school bus and booking down the road for some reason or another. On the news, nobody in his town looked surprised. At first, Mom and I were a tiny bit shocked until we heard that the boy was from Arkansas; then it made all the sense in the world. Mom said, "Well, I bet he's been driving a tractor forever. School bus's not that different."

We're not exactly country the same way that school-bus-stealing kid is, or I'm not, but Mom hasn't been able to get the country all the way out of herself. That's why I'm a good a driver. Thanks to Mom, I've been driving around for forty percent of my life; this is no problem for me.

I'll obey the speed limit and stay awake. I will keep breathing and make a plan to keep myself from freaking out. Everything is ready; I've packed only one suitcase with my favorite jeans, a swimsuit, and a few T-shirts. Anything else I need I can find in Wren. The little cooler is packed with ice, water, and cranberry juice. Being highly susceptible to bladder infections makes cranberry juice mandatory.

I know how to drive, I know the way, and I am going to Wren.

I feel sure that my Lucky Jeans, which didn't help me out at school, will bring me luck now. For starters, although the moon is not quite full, it's just what I need for backing out of the driveway with no lights on — bright and round, with no cloudy interference, and high enough above the trees that it's casting down right on the driveway. I couldn't ask for a more cooperative sky.

At the top of our hill, I push the truck a few steps to get it moving. My hands are sweating up a storm, and my Ayma spot itches. I keep the lights off and roll away from the house so Mom doesn't wake up. Midway down our hill, with no regret or hesitation, I do it. I press in the clutch, shift into second, and pop the clutch out. No big deal—the engine starts right up; I am on my own.

I pull into the first gas station I see to fill up. I have thirty dollars and Mom's credit card in my back pocket. In case Mom cancels the card after she wakes up and finds me gone, I use the card first. My heart is pounding so hard that I can feel my pulse in my wrist and in my temples. I lean against the truck and think.

I love this truck. I wipe my clammy palms on my jeans and slide myself behind the wheel. Holding on to the dashboard, for just a minute, I make my plan. I'm taller than Mom and I can see out the windows fine. At this time of night, the roads will be freer of traffic—just the truckers and me all the way to Alabama. I know the way, and once I get into Tennessee, there are shortcuts to Wren. There's nothing left for me to do now except drive for six hundred ninety-one miles or forget it and drive home.

The truck smells like feet: I put down the windows to let some fresh air in and to keep me awake. Mom will be fuming mad in the morning when she wakes up. I can't think about Mom; I scratch my left calf.

I remember how at Ayma's, in the spare bedroom upstairs, where we spend the night, there is always that cross breeze that Ayma loves to bring in by opening the east and west windows. I can even almost hear the Wren cicadas that take over at night. We have lots of cicadas here, but the Wren cicadas could never be outdone by ours. Sometimes, the cicadas are so loud at Ayma's that I'm scared to step outside. I have been assaulted by a cicada at Ayma's, but it didn't mean any harm; I just got in its way.

This is so easy. I turn on the radio because I am tired of silence. I want music and voices all the way to Wren. Whether it's country music or a preacher telling me how to get right with the Lord, I want someone's voice keeping me company and keeping the truck filled up. There has been enough silence.

Every station sucks at three in the morning; every channel gets on my nerves. I'm finding sports, crazy-annoying jazz, and, of course, there is plenty of preaching. Once I get to Roanoke, I might find nothing but preaching on the radio. I'm too nervous to keep messing with the dial while I drive, so I settle for Top Forty. Mom would be gagging.

I am gagging, too, until they play that dumb, stupid song about the beautiful girl who is a disaster—the girl who would change herself for the world to love her. Or whatever—I hate that song.

I hate that song so much that I crank the radio all the way up and I think I close my eyes, even though I'm driving, because Drew Walker did put his hand on the small of my back once and this song was playing. Yes, he did. I'm sure it happened, though the why of it is the thing that I have forgotten.

There was a day, last October, when Mom came to school and told all of the sixth-grade classes about her job. She told everyone about being a forest ranger, and everyone listened. She passed around a rattle from a twenty-year-old timber rattler and talked about the poisonous snakes of Virginia. She taught the girls how to tie a half hitch and then she lassoed Drew Walker, even though she's a ranger, not a cowboy. Her face turned all beety and blotchy, but I still bet I'm the only one who knew exactly how nervous she really was.

That day, nobody threw milk at me or shoved me into my locker or whispered funny names. Mom, who has an aversion to people that is almost as bad as mine, knows how to pretend better than I do. She pretended that she loved everyone and they loved her, too, and they left me alone for one day. That day was the happiest day of my life.

The same day that Mom drove me home in October

was our middle-school fall dance, and that night at the dance Drew Walker picked me.

Mom had bought me these very same Lucky Jeans that I am wearing now and a pink lace cami, with full coverage, from Abercrombie, that I will never wear again because that's where he touched me. I had straightened my hair. I looked so pretty, and when I walked into the gym, everyone turned to look at me. No one laughed. No one pointed, either, and on the first slow song — this she's-a-disaster-and-she's-beautiful song that is blasting through the truck's speakers now — Drew Walker held me. He placed his hand in the middle of my back and guided me out to dance. He didn't ask me; he took me and I went. I went because I am a foolish girl.

CHAPTER SEVEN

I THINK SOMETIMES when you keep your eyes closed for too long it's because you hope for real magic, just like in real fairy tales. Mom banned fairy tales from our house, so I only ever watched them at Krystal's house. I've read every fairy tale at the library, too. While I was dancing with Drew, I didn't exactly think I would open my eyes to a ball gown or a pumpkin coach or a pair of footmen who were really mice. I wasn't chanting bibbity-bobbity under my breath. If nothing changed at all and I could have just had those few seconds to keep forever, that would have been magic enough for me. When I closed my eyes for the ten or twenty seconds that I did, though, I made reverse magic.

Drew and I sort of swayed and I kept my eyes shut. While I was swaying there, the moon was on my mind. I remember that the moon that night was pale orange and one hundred percent full. Mom had driven the river road to the dance, especially so we could see that orange moon filling up the dark blue sky over our river. Drew and I didn't say one word. I was smiling and wishing I could show him the moon or bring it inside. Maybe there were even a few orange balloons, the same color as the moon, on the gym floor. There were probably balloons and streamers hanging from the ceiling.

He pressed his hand into my pink cami. I had not expected Drew's hand to be sweaty; he sweated through my shirt. Maybe I shut my eyes because I knew I didn't want to see.

The same song was still playing when I opened my eyes, but the dance had stopped. All the laughing and pointing started then—just later than I had expected. I looked so pretty that night. I mean, I looked so pretty that I looked like somebody else. The problem is they all knew it was me.

I snap the radio off and by myself, in the truck, I sing the lyrics over and over. When I get to the part about changing it all to be happy forever, I start to feel brave, then scared. What if you can't change a disaster — even a beautiful one? What if I am the girl in that song?

I sing loud.

I put everything I have into it for the next three hours all the way to Roanoke. For the first one hundred times through the song, I can't stop crying. My gray hoodie is covered in one hundred sixty miles' worth of tears and snot. I pretty much stay in the right-hand lane, downshifting only when the grade of the Virginia mountains forces me to change gears.

I keep the radio off and keep the windows up so nothing can get in and nothing can get out without my invitation. By the time I get to Abingdon, I have driven through the night, but I'm still in Virginia and not quite halfway to Ayma's. It's seven thirty a.m.; I am hoarse, tired, and out of gas. I fill up one more time and again lean against the dash to make a plan for the second half of my trip. I need supplies: coffee, a fruit bar, and water for later.

I belt out the happy-ever-after song until I am out of Virginia, and then I make a promise to myself. I'm not singing that song ever again. When I hit Tennessee, where the speed limit is seventy, I push the truck to seventy-five and blow right on past Exit 398 because I have lost my taste for tiny cheeseburgers with a girl's name.

The truck smells good now, like mountain air. I decide I need new sounds, sounds that match the smell of this mountain air, sounds that will take me to Ayma's.

So I sing all new songs. I sing Edie Brickell and Ray, and then I sing Johnny Cash and Bruce. As soon as I get into Alabama, I think about singing that song the Drive-By Truckers wrote just for Highway 72. But I don't sing it. I have made it all the way here, I am thankful, and this highway's not mean. I am going home to Ayma. Instead I sing Ayma's song, "His Eye Is on the Sparrow," for the rest of the way to Wren.

Chapter Eight

BEFORE NOW, for my whole life, whenever Mom and I have come back here, we first off would drive around the town square in Moulton, to see how everything has changed. If Mom were with me now, we would ride around the square looking at the courthouse, checking out the Merle Norman store and wondering why it's about the only store that has managed to survive on the square. We might pull up and buy blueberries and boiled peanuts from a farmer.

Today I speed through Moulton and only come to a rolling stop at the square. I have come all this way to get to one house, and I'm in a hurry to see one person. I will have as many days as I need to visit the square.

Everyone says the land between Moulton and Wren is developed, but it's not developed compared to the miles and miles of side-by-side black and beige houses in Virginia. Here, you can tell people still farm. There are more houses, for sure, but nearly all of them have a field of corn or soy or a pasture of cows for a front yard. I pass the Pine Grove Baptist Church and the old gas station right at Wren, where Alabama 33 and 36 intersect. There is still no stoplight, only a stop sign.

Wren used to have its own post office, but now it's all rolled up with Moulton's. These days, though, Wren is nothing but a gas station that doesn't even let you swipe a credit card at the pump. It's not the same Wren that Ayma talks about, with men dragging fields and women trading at the general store. There's a café called Evelyn's that runs its business out of the garage, with two picnic tables out front. You have to watch for the spray-painted sign that Evelyn herself props up on a card table, BBQ AND GREENS NOW! Then you know it's time for lunch at Evelyn's. The sign is out, but as good as I know that barbecue will be, I step on the gas.

I have forgotten Wren. Coming into Wren, from Moulton Valley, it surprises me to look around and see that I have yet to leave the mountains. From every direction in Wren, I still see the Smokies on the horizon. Though Wren gives the Great Smoky Mountains their westernmost foothills, they kind of sneak up on you. I always forget.

Here is what I mean about Wren being deceiving. I drive up what feels like a small hill with an almost unnoticeable grade. The land changes right away. I downshift to second gear and look at everything; this is my home. Now I am back thick in the mountains, and thick in the woods where, according to Ayma's family Bible, our family has lived since before this land was even a state. I'm sure the land was an older, different forest when our family first showed up. I put my head all the way out the window to smell the forest and to smell Wren Mountain, too.

The forest here, at the roadside, is not all hardwood and it's not all that old, either. Even I can tell that these trees are young, because some of their trunks are no thicker than my thighs. I can pick out a few trees from the leaves: the tulip poplar's leaves are shaped like a tulip, and even the sapling leaves are wider than my face. Oak is easy enough for me to spot, too, though I'd have to look up which kind.

Of course it's easier when they're blooming, but I can

tell redbuds easy by their heart-shaped leaves. Dogwoods and cedar trees grow like weeds in Virginia, so I more or less know them on sight. The dogwoods seem all spindly-looking in the woods, and the cedars, if you tune your eyes right, appear like feathers in the forest. Everybody knows a pine tree when they see it, but only weird people like Mom really know enough to distinguish which pine is which.

Ayma lives inside the boundaries of the Black Warrior Forest. When it was first designated a national forest, way back in the 1930s, Ayma was just born. Her people had been living here for a hundred and forty years by that time. At the towering brown sign that announces the Black Warrior Forest, I turn right onto a gravel road with no name and no number. This is Ayma's road, and it's a steeper climb, about two miles up the road to the house.

Ayma's house sits at the very top of Wren Mountain, exactly the way I remember. Her old, white, four-square house still has its shiny red-tin roof. There is not a flake or hint of old in the paint; Ayma keeps her place looking clean and well groomed, same as she is herself. A screen porch built onto the front of the house faces the road. The real front of the house, where no one ever enters, faces the valley. Ayma owns more than six hundred acres out here, most of it open cow pasture, surrounded by the Black Warrior Forest on all sides except the side that faces Moulton Valley.

I turn in the drive lined by poplar trees that must be nearing one hundred years old. I jump out, leaving the keys in the ignition. The gravel dust that I've stirred up from coming too fast up the road swirls in my nose and makes me sneeze. I can taste it like chalk in my mouth.

As I stand here in Ayma's yard, everything I wanted to remember rushes into me. I feel like I have found something that I lost so long ago that I buried it inside me until this very moment and now with Wren, again, here in front of me and all around me, I remember. All at once, Wren is new and familiar.

Ayma's cows, mostly Black Angus, graze in the two fields across the road. A few are in the paddock beside the house, next to the barn. I figure these cows are new arrivals and Ayma has them parked over there, letting them acclimate before she turns them out with the rest of the herd.

"Here she is!" Ayma rushes to greet me, wiping her hands on her pants.

She stretches up on her tippy toes to see eye to eye with me, but I have outgrown her. Ayma is an itty bitty thing; Mom is just like her. She hugs me for a long time without saying a word. I know from how she scoops me with both arms and presses her cheek into my face that Mom has already called her. My grandmother is the first one to speak: "You are precious, Mary Harold. You are my precious child. You are gon' be just fine with me. I'm gon' take good care of you."

I wrap my arms all the way around Ayma's tiny waist and hold on to her, not saying a word. I can kiss the top of her head without having to stretch up like I had to when I was little. I almost have to stoop down.

"My beauty," Ayma says, "I've been praying all night, and here you are safe, lovely, and soaring over me like one of these here poplar trees. I am so happy to see you." My little grandmother hugs me so tight that I feel all of her strength running directly into me.

"Um-um," she sings like she has tasted something sweet, but it's only me that is so sweet to her.

"I had my phone on, Ayma," I reassure her. "I would have picked up." I wonder if she tried to call but I was singing too loud in the truck.

"I'm sure you would have picked up. Bad enough that a thirteen-year-old stole her mother's car and drove it across the South without a license, don't you think? Do I want that child talking on the phone and driving at the same time? I think not. I knew you were coming here.

The Lord was gon' do better overseeing that journey than I was, anyhow. Let's go inside and talk."

Ayma goes on ahead of me.

I lag behind, watching all the white butterflies dance around Ayma's daylilies. I want to run fast, then stop quick and sit in the lilies, being still as a statue like I did when I was four and see if the butterflies would land on me now. I remember how once they did rest on me, and I believe they would again, if maybe only for a second. Instead of running and stopping, though, I ask for something.

"Ayma, remember how we used to always give butterfly kisses?"

She comes back and, saying nothing, brings her eyelashes extra close to my cheek; we are nearly touching. I shut my eyes and wait for the ticklish kiss I remember. The baby-fine hairs of Ayma's face reach out to me, and her eyelashes flutter so, so softly against my face. They flutter me again then, and I butterfly-kiss her, too. Before I do anything else, I want for just these couple of more minutes the freedom to imagine my brand-new life.

Chapter Nine

⁓

INSIDE, THE HOUSE IS ALL SILENT, just holding its breath, it seems, for me to come inside. I set my one suitcase down in the hall. I think I should call Mom to let her know I'm here. She's probably a little bit worried, even though she never called me once, and would at least like to know I'm safe. My chest tightens; I try to make myself take a breath, but every time I do, the pinch gets stronger.

I call out for help. "Ayma?"

She knows me, too. Maybe not in the same way as Mom does, but Ayma knows me. I got my leg spot from her, so we're the same. Right away she is beside me, telling me, "Mary Harold, you're gon' be fine. You're strong; you're a survivor. All the women in our family are strong."

I tilt my face straight up to the ceiling. Ayma's crown molding is perfect; there's not a crack in it. She's so proud of the crown molding. Every room in the house has it. I open my mouth and take one deep breath to fill my lungs. I think how sweet of Ayma that she was praying for me all night. I like knowing that while I was driving by myself on the dark highway, Ayma was awake praying just for me.

I stop breathing.

"Ayma? You were up all night praying for me?"

She pats me. "I surely was. Not just me, either. I called up my women friends from the Baptist church to join me. I know there were angels all around you."

"Oh." Had they all been praying all night? I wonder. "When did Mom call you? I left at —"

"Now, come on back to the kitchen," Ayma interrupts. "You've got a visitor been waiting to see you."

I stop cold in the hallway. "Mom?"

"Uh-huh. Got here just about thirty minutes ahead of you. Drove her car behind the barn and been sitting, waiting patiently for you."

"No way! She was asleep when I left." This totally sucks.

Ayma looks at me with a whole lot of sympathy and sort of pats me on the back and shakes her head like she might be thinking I'm sort of pathetic in that way that grown-ups do sometimes.

"Experience, desperation, and an electric car that gets sixty miles to the gallon—that's a whale of a good hand, my dear. Go take your lumps." Ayma takes my hand, kisses it, then holds my hand up. "See? I got you now. We're gon' figure this out. Come on."

Almost before I can sit down, Mom starts telling Ayma and me her rules. She offers me no hug, no hello, no eye contact—nothing.

"First of all, Mary Harold needs a cow of her own," Mom says to Ayma. Then Mom turns to me. "If you're going to live here, you need to be a part of things. Lord knows, you need to have a purpose, something that interests you. Working on the farm will be good for you."

"I'll see to it that Bud gets a good gentle cow for you," Ayma tells me. Mom shoots Ayma a look and opens her mouth to protest.

Ayma doesn't respond to Mom's sassy face but instead nods her on with the rules. "Fine, Bye." Not just Ayma, but everyone in Wren calls Mom "Bye." Her full name is Tabythia, but I've never heard her called that. "What else?"

"Second, there will be no dragging Mary Harold to

church every Wednesday and Sunday. That about did me in, Mother. If she wants to go to church with you, that's fine, but you may not make her go. Whatever else you want to do on Sunday—rest, read, sin, walk the old trails—is fine, but she is not to be forced into church." Ayma winks at me and just blinks her agreement to Mom.

"Third"—Mom directs this rule to me—"Mary Harold, I'll end this experiment in a flash if I feel you are not happy or are not thriving.

"Fourth, I need to hear from you every week by phone, and it would help me sleep better to hear from you every day for a while."

Ayma nods again. "I've got the e-mail, Bye. Bud taught me how to use the e-mail, bought me a computer for my birthday. I'm too busy to use it a lot." This annoys Mom to no end.

"Are you kidding me? Why haven't you ever e-mailed me?"

Ayma is so innocent. "Now, Bye, don't get nervy with me. I use the e-mail with people I don't care to see or meet, to attend to my business. You are not one of those people. You are someone who I want to touch and see and smell."

Mom can't stand it anymore and corrects Ayma: "Anyway, Mother, it's not called *the e-mail*; it's called *e-mail*. There's no article before *e-mail*. And fifth, let's get one thing straight about Bud—"

Ayma cuts Mom off before she can finish her tirade about the rules. "Bye, you are odd. I carried you in my womb, brought you into the world, and raised you up. Now here you come with all kinds of rules for me, and correcting my grammar like there's no tomorrow. Mary Harold is welcome to live here with me—you know you are, too—for as long as either or both of you want to do so. Both of you are precious to me; I am so proud of you both."

Ayma strokes Mom's cheek and says quietly, "No one is gon' tell you how to raise Mary Harold, love, certainly not me. Besides, you're doing a fine job on your own; you surely are."

Mom closes her eyes. "I'm sorry, Mama. This is hard."

"Bye, you are not a failure. You are a mother trying to do right by her child. There is nothing harder. I know from experience." Ayma cups Mom's chin in her hand. "She's your girl, Bye—that's all."

Then Mom crumbles into Ayma's arms as if she's the runaway girl and not my mom or anybody's mom at all. She almost begs Ayma: "Mother, I don't know what to do right now. Can you help me?"

Ayma shushes Mom like a tiny baby and draws her

fingers all across Mom's face and hair. For a second it feels like Ayma has forgotten I'm here, too, but she hasn't really, because she grabs my hand and hooks it with Mom's hand. "Here she is; here she is, Bye. You tell *her.* You tell your baby girl what's on your heart."

I hold Mom's hand tight, in a death grip, wanting to take care of her like I do when she comes home so tired from working in the Pocahontas Forest. But I wait until Mom looks up into my face. Mom's brown eyes find mine and hold them for the longest time.

She whispers so softly that I have to bend down to hear. "Cricket, I will stick with you. I promise."

I find her eyes and make a picture of Mom because I know that as soon as she's gone, I'll want to remember everything: her square face, her wispy short hair with that cowlick in her part, and these coonhound eyes. I'll have to remember, too, that her leaving me here is her way of sticking with me.

Chapter Ten

I MEET MY COW AND BUD ON FRIDAY, the very next morning. Ayma, Mom, and I wait on the screen porch for Bud to return from Cullman, where they have a cattle auction every week. Bud Hale is Ayma's farm manager, if you could call it that, since this farm is not big enough for a full-time farm manager. I've heard Ayma talk about him a few times on the phone.

The Hales have lived in Lawrence County for even longer than our family has, only Bud has just in the last year moved up here on Wren Mountain next to Ayma. Like a lot of farmers, Bud works his farm and does other work, too. His big thing, though, is running for office. Ayma says Bud is a perennial candidate for the Lawrence County Board of Supervisors.

Mom is unhappy that Ayma sent Bud to Cullman, even though Mom's number-one rule for me staying here in Wren is having my own cow.

"Bud's so smug. I mean, he can be such an ass," Mom says with a pout.

Ayma refuses to participate in that kind of talk. "My foot, Bye, grow up. If you're not over him after all these years, you never will be. Bud is loyal and true, and he takes care of this farm. I'll not change the way I act because you're ashamed of yourself."

I know Mom is tired from the drive, but there's something wrong with her today. Not only did she swear in front of Ayma, but her hair has, like, product in it. She thinks I can't tell. And then Mom is the first one to notice the gravel cloud moving toward us. She's sure that it's Bud. We're all sure that it's Bud.

At 11:30 a.m. sharp, right when he said he would, Bud pulls up. Mom is the first one off the porch to greet him, only they don't actually greet each other like normal people. They sort of toss heads at each other, and without talking, Mom picks up a cattle prod from the grass while Bud unloads the prettiest black cow I have ever seen. I see her through the sides of the trailer, and she is fine.

Mom must think Bud is still pretty fine, too, because she keeps swallowing over and over—a sure sign that she is coming undone at the sight of him. Even though Bud's face is hidden by a ball cap pushed way down over his eyes, he looks pretty much how I expected him to look from the way Mom and Ayma have been talking. Lots of straight, black hair sticks through the back of his cap. About any man looks tall next to Mom and Ayma; Bud's pretty much a giant next to both of them. The sun has turned him chestnut.

Mom hasn't spoken a word since seeing Bud; maybe the heat is getting to her. The temperature is one hundred three degrees outside according to the thermometer on the barn door, which is in the shade. We're all three standing under a poplar tree, while Bud unloads my cow into the paddock behind Ayma's barn, where there is not a lick of shade. Standing in the full sun, my cow is as shiny black as the shoes I wore when I was little. She starts eating grass right away, like she is glad to have come home. She is sweet, I think. I name her Sue, my sweet Sue.

Bud tells me that he took his time, seeking out the gentlest cow he could find. At Cullman, he saw Sue standing away from the other cows in her lot. Bud called out to her, "Would you like to be a young girl's first cow?" The way Bud tells it, she walked right over to him.

Bud wants Sue and me to get acquainted with each other before we turn her out with the rest of the herd. I think Mom wants to hurry up this process; she stands at the gate with her arms folded across her chest. Bud is in no hurry at all. He takes his hat off and rubs his hand through his black hair.

Bud is not one of those early receders, like the one and only man I know of who took Mom out on a date. That guy didn't stand a chance, not because of his hairline but because Mom is just not cut out for dating. I personally think that it's this guy Bud who ruined Mom for dating anybody else—so he is on my watch list. We'll see about him.

Though we have not been formally introduced, Bud speaks to me directly: "Mary Harold, come on over here and meet your cow."

I walk toward Bud, but too quickly; Sue takes a step back. Bud holds up a hand to stop me. "Did I tell you already that Sue's bred back? Look at her good; see how big she is? I think any day now you'll have a calf to tend."

He looks over his shoulder at Mom. "Didn't I do good, Bye?" I think that is Bud's way of flirting with Mom. She ignores him.

I talk to Bud to take some heat off of Mom. "Cool, so 'bred back' means she's already pregnant with a calf? Will I get to see the calf be born?"

Bud hand-signals me to stand still. "You're gon' see plenty of births. I got half a dozen cows ready to drop today. You can help me; I been telling your grandmother we need another hand around here, anyway.

"Move out kind of slow. Keep your head looking down," he directs me. "That's right. Now watch her body language; she'll tell you when she's ready for you to come closer." Bud waves me forward slowly, like he's a traffic cop.

Mom, being sarcastic, asks, "You fancy yourself a cow whisperer, Bud?"

When she is not ignoring him, she gets all rude. It's getting on my nerves that she can't even be civil. And for another thing, it is driving me crazy that she is talking funny. Mom never says things like "fancy yourself" or "Lord knows." She's talking like Ayma.

"Bud, pay that girl no mind. Keep on about your business with Mary Harold," orders Ayma.

Bud doesn't hear either one of them. He stays focused on Sue and me getting to know each other. I do as Bud asks me. Keeping my head down, I slowly move toward my cow.

"Good, good, good. Now, put your hand out."

I stretch out my hand; Sue takes half a step backward.

Bud is determined that Sue and I make friends quickly. "Can you touch your toes?" he asks.

"Sure."

"Okay, do it and just hang there for as long as it takes."

I bend over, touch my toes, and let my hands swing through the clover, being watchful for bees. I put my palms flat out on the ground, stretching my calves out good. I touch my nose to my knees. Sue steps closer and lowers her head. Bud orders me again, in a whisper, "Now, squat down so you're real low."

I squat and tuck my head into my knees. In a few seconds, Sue walks right up to me, smells my hair, and then licks my neck twice. Her black tongue startles me; it's so rough, like sandpaper, but I don't move when she licks me. I let Sue get to know me.

My ponytail falls off to the side, and I feel the sun heating up my bare neck. We belong to each other now. Sue is my cow, and I guess I'm her girl.

"All right, Miss Mary Harold, you done good. I think if you keep spending time with her, getting to know her, you'll have a true friend in Sue," Bud tells me.

Bud shows me how to put grain out for her. She seems to know that the white plastic bucket is meant for her, and she comes right over to the trough with me. Never in my life have I been this close to such a big animal.

Sue's eyes are the color of Mom's and shaped like almonds, with eyelashes so long that most females of the human species would pay lots of money to have these on their own faces. Every now and then Sue moos right at my face like she wants me to get her something. I figure she might want more grain, so I reach in the white bucket and give her another good handful, which quiets her. I still can't get over that black tongue. I guess I am too used to tongues being pink or red.

Bud stands in between Mom and Ayma on the other side of the fence from me. Poor Mom is so nervous-looking that I am beyond wanting to laugh at her; I almost can't stand to watch her. Her face and neck are splotching up, and not from the heat. Bud's not nervous-looking at all. He leans over the fence, watching Sue and me. I see him turn his head to Mom and speak. Mom doesn't look directly at Bud; I can't tell if she even says a word.

As much as I've been judging Mom's manners, I have forgotten my own. I tell Sue good-bye and run over to the fence. I hold my hand out, like Mom has taught me to do, and look directly at Bud. He's sort of cute the way he is standing there close to Mom, acting unaware that he's right up in her personal space.

"Thank you for bringing me Sue and helping me get to know her. I appreciate your taking the time," I tell him.

Bud takes my hand and shakes it firmly, like we're doing real business. "Glad to do it. Your mama and your grandmother are fine ladies—two of my favorites. I have a daughter, too, you know. She's a bit younger than you are, but she could show you around Wren. You come on by anytime, and you two can ride horses or go swimming in the Sipsey River."

That sounds great to me. Before I can say anything, Ayma speaks up. "I have an even better idea! I believe we just missed Mary Harold's thirteenth birthday last month." Mom and I nod at the same time.

"Let's have a party! Bud, why don't you bring Dixie and Delta over for supper tomorrow night? Tomorrow is Bye's last night with us; we'll have a birthday party and a welcoming party all rolled into one."

Bud looks at Mom, asking with his eyes if it's okay. Mom looks like she is going to pass out. She swallows real hard and gives Bud a faint little nod of her head.

That's all Bud needs. "Sounds like a plan. We'll be here. I'll make sure I get Delta in the tub before then; that boy's a mess."

The last time I had a party in my honor was in the fourth grade; I'm thinking maybe I do belong here in Wren.

CHAPTER ELEVEN

EARLY THIS MORNING, while it was still dark out, I woke up peeing blood. I get bladder infections a lot because I hold my pee for too long and also, Ayma's right, because I forget to drink enough water. Usually I can tell when I am getting a new one because of the stinging, though this one has taken me by surprise. I can barely walk. If I just sit on the toilet and try to pee, it feels a little better, but I cannot sit on the toilet all day long. I've got my birthday party tonight.

Ayma insists I need to see the doctor, so she calls Dr. Jeter at home because he keeps Saturday hours at the county clinic. When Ayma tells him that I have blood in my urine, and because Ayma asks him nicely, and because they are old friends, he is willing to squeeze me in first thing, without an appointment.

Mom is taking me to the clinic, and, of course, Ayma makes us take her car because she likes to keep it charged. Mom flaps a little before agreeing to take Ayma's car because she thinks people will recognize it. Mom's nervous we'll bump into folks who think we're Ayma and they'll get all worked up for a chat in the street. Exchanging news with one another is a big hobby in Wren.

Wren is small enough that it's only natural that everybody knows all your business all of the time. Everybody here knows everything about everybody. Mom can't forget that part of living in Wren; she hates it. She never could get used to her private business being public business. Some people, like Ayma, aren't bothered by nosiness. Ayma even likes her business being broadcast around the county. I think it makes her feel safe and belonging someplace. If there is one place in Lawrence County to broadcast your business, it has to be the Lawrence County Medical Clinic, which is located right next to the post office. The whole county, seems like, is always either at one place or the other.

Before we even open Ayma's car door, I think Mom's

wishing she were back in Virginia. Mom is extra-sensitive about people judging her, for a lot of reasons that she won't talk about. All rolled up into one, I think they are all the same reason—she didn't act like Wren girls are supposed to act. Wren feels like home to me, though, and I wish somehow Wren could be home to Mom again, too.

As soon as we park, a swarm of Baptist ladies buzzing around the post office buzzes over to the car, looking for Ayma. Before long the ladies realize that we're not with Ayma; we're just driving her car. All they want, anyway, is some juicy details of something besides themselves; it doesn't faze them one bit that we're not Ayma.

"Hey there, Bye. Are you all coming to the post office or the clinic?" one of them asks.

I can see that Mom doesn't want to answer. But she does. "Mary Harold's not feeling very well. We're going to see Dr. Jeter," she tells them, and then apologizes to me with her eyes.

"Oh, I am sorry to hear that, darlin'," says the lady with the rolled-down stockings.

They all wait for Mom to fill them in with the full scoop of what's wrong with me. I imagine they want some details of me driving by myself, too, since I know straight from Ayma's mouth that she did, in fact, call up some of her Baptist friends in the middle of the night to get them praying for me. I figure these Baptist ladies standing before me are the very ones Ayma woke in the middle of the night to pray for my safe journey while I was singing Edie and Bruce Springsteen all the way home. I guess I owe them thanks.

After too long of a silence and Mom not offering up a thing, a different Baptist lady asks her straight up, "Well, what's wrong?"

Mom refuses to answer. She takes my hand and very politely says, "Excuse us, y'all—we're late."

Just as we're rushing off to see Dr. Jeter, the stockings lady calls out to me personally, "Mary Harold?"

I can't help myself; I turn to her because I live here now and I want to be friendly. Mom yanks hard on my belt loop to pull me back, but I shake my butt at her to wave her off. I live in Wren now, not Mom.

Stockings lady takes my hand in hers. "You don't remember me, hon. Your grandmother and I go way back. My name is Madilee Simms. I know this will be a definite time of adjustment for you, being away from your mama and all. I just want you to know that I'll be praying for you." Madilee pecks me on the cheek. Then she tells Mom, "You, too, Bye. I'll be praying for you, too."

At the clinic everything goes like I knew it would. Of course, I have a bladder infection. I had already figured that out myself, without needing to pee in a cup. I should have stopped to go to the bathroom more when I was running away; I was nervous, though, that I would get caught driving without a license. Because of the blood, Dr. Jeter calls it hemorrhaging cystitis instead of plain old cystitis like I usually get.

After the clinic, we walk to the drugstore to get my medicine. Due to the pain, I am most interested in not wasting another minute. The drugstore is around the corner from the clinic, and there we run into more ladies who know Ayma and Mom. These ladies had run into the first swarm of ladies, so they are just following up to see if I am all right.

Truthfully, I think they have been staking us out so they can be the first ones with the info. We avoid more questions about what is wrong with me. They all seem to know that I am going to be living here, so they all ask to hug me. Well, they actually don't ask; they sort of boss me.

"Come here and let me squeeze your neck."

"Oooh, you look as sweet as ever!"

"When I first met you, you were a little thing."

Soft, jiggly arms are flying from every which way, grabbing onto me so tight like they've really missed me. I don't mind jiggly arms hugging me. I don't mind the smallness of Wren so much, either. Nobody says a word about the sketchy circumstances of my arrival in Wren, and I am relieved.

Still, I was wrong to expect I might get some privacy with my bladder. Even as we walk in the door back home, Ayma is on the phone gabbing about the blood in my urine. I hear her say, "Well, she has blood in her urine. Oh, it's painful. You can't imagine how painful it is. She went uptown to see Dr. Jeter. Oh, wait a minute. Here she is. Let me ask her."

"Well, what did the doctor say?" Ayma cups her hand over the phone and asks me.

Before Mom can intervene, I blurt out, "He said I have *hemorrhaging* cystitis," purposefully exaggerating the hemorrhaging part, hoping for extra sympathy from Ayma.

When Ayma reports directly back to her phone pal, Louisa, she listens again, then says, "You're right. Well, hold on, now. I'll ask her that."

This time Ayma doesn't bother covering the phone up; she practically hollers at me, "Precious, do you wipe from front to back? Because if you don't, that's one way you can get infected, if you bring the bacteria from the back to the front."

Ayma demonstrates what she means by air-wiping front to back and then back to front. She is not at all bothered about asking me this.

Ayma makes impatient eyes at me when I don't answer. "Well?"

"Ayma, gross! That's so gross! Of course I wipe from front to back! I don't drink enough water, that's all."

Mom raises her eyebrows at me and smirks a little bit. She doesn't have to say anything; I know she means for me to get it that if I can't handle people asking about my most private business, then Wren is not the place for me. I raise my eyebrows double-strong back at her with my own message: I can *handle* it.

The morning goes pretty much like this—ladies calling or coming over to be sure I know to wipe from front to back. Ayma's lady friends, including those we ran into in town, make the drive up Wren Mountain, just to drop by the house to check on me. Ayma even brings out the silver tea service, which she keeps polished on the dining-room sideboard. "Might as well use it every now and again," she reasons.

Here I am with six old ladies, plus Mom, sitting in the kitchen talking about female problems. Somehow we manage to all squeeze in around the kitchen table. I am picking up that around here, talk about your private affairs is no big deal and each one of us is expected to pitch in with a story. Soon enough everybody's laughing and carrying on.

Ayma hollers out, "We're having a hen party! No roosters allowed!" That makes everybody howl.

Louisa counts us all one by one and includes me, too, then announces, "Eight hens! That's a pretty good hen party."

Then somebody else shouts out again, "No roosters allowed! Uh-huh!" Even Mom cracks up; I like seeing Mom laugh, so that makes me laugh, and soon we're all laughing so hard at the stupid rooster joke that tears are running down all our faces.

Then Louisa gets back to the female stories and recalls thinking her water broke with her first child when she was eight months pregnant, but she had only wet herself. Mom laughs at that story, too. I know she wouldn't admit it, but sitting here with these ladies talking today has helped Mom. She is calmer, and she is even managing to smile a lot. When Madilee, still wearing those stockings rolled down, cries a little at the memory of having had a hysterectomy at the age of thirty-five, after three miscarriages and no children, we all get real quiet.

And then Mom whispers, "I am leaving my daughter here in Wren. Please take care of her. *Please.*" All the ladies gather around Mom and hold her tight. I hold her tight, too.

CHAPTER TWELVE

BY THE TIME OF MY BIRTHDAY and Welcome-to-Wren dinner, I have peed through enough medicine that my bladder pain has dulled a good deal. A cold front came through today, bringing the high only to eighty-five, so Ayma has turned off the AC and thrown open all of the windows. Lying here on my bed with the ceiling fan sucking that breeze in off of Wren Mountain and twirling it all around my room is making me practically drool myself to sleep.

I French-braided my hair for my party; it's long enough that I can drape the braid over my right shoulder and it almost touches my breast. Mom bought me a dress in Moulton this morning, especially for tonight. I don't expect to wear a dress again until sometime next year, possibly, if we have a party for me again, when I turn fourteen.

Right underneath my room, I hear Mom and Ayma giggling together downstairs in the kitchen. I close my eyes and wish that all of this was my real and permanent life. When I think of Mom leaving, my chest starts hurting. I am already so far away from the life I left back there that a tiny slice of my heart is tugging at me to go back with Mom. All those people, all those reasons for leaving, now seem like clouds in the sky that would blow right on by if I stretched out on a blanket and watched for long enough.

Outside, below my window, a little voice in the yard growls, "Stop messing with my hair!"

Then I hear Bud say, "Settle down, champ."

Before they can ring the bell, I fly down the stairs, intending to shout into the kitchen at Mom and Ayma on my way to answering the door.

"Mom? Oh, my God. You have a dress on. And makeup," is all I can think to say when I practically run into Mom at the bottom of the stairs.

Her face falls in an instant. "I knew this was a mistake," she says. "I haven't worn a dress or makeup in twenty years. Heaven knows what possessed me to start now. Is it too late for me to change clothes?"

She looks prettier than ever, wearing one of her old dresses, a faded yellow-and-white sundress that swishes around her. The dress still fits just exactly right.

"No! I mean, no, don't change. You look great, honest. And the bare feet are perfect; you look kind of casual, like you don't care that you're not all the way dressed." I kick my shoes off, too, as my way of sticking with Mom.

The doorbell rings, and a look of panic washes over her. She swallows in her nervous way.

I kiss her cheek and tell her, "You're the prettiest mom on earth. I'll get the door."

Bud looks equally uncomfortable, wearing clean jeans and a fancy blue shirt with satin ribbon across the chest and trailing over his shoulders. I might not have recognized him without his cap, though he has on the same dirty boots.

Standing too close behind Bud are the two I've been waiting to meet—Dixie and Delta. Bud pushes a handful of black-eyed Susans toward me. "For the birthday girl," he says.

Little bugs and green spiders are still crawling all over the flowers. I hand them to Mom since she's used to dealing with insects.

Bud pulls his daughter beside him. "Bye, Mary Harold, I'd like y'all to meet my daughter, Dixie."

I smile at Dixie the way Mom taught me, full in the face. When our eyes meet, I smile. I smile like a girl; Dixie doesn't smile at all. She tosses her head and whinnies, like a horse.

Mom offers her hand to Dixie. "I'm Bye, an old friend of your dad's. Nice to meet you, Miss Dixie."

Dixie doesn't say a word to Mom; she turns completely away from her.

"Dixie . . ." Bud starts explaining, "Dixie has a kind of different way of communicating." Then he rubs her hair and says sweetly to her, "We're working on that, aren't we?"

Dixie brushes him off and runs outside to the yard.

A tiny boy with jet-black hair in a crew cut, wearing a plaid shirt like he is somebody's granddaddy, pops his head out from behind Bud. "Don't pay her no attention. She thinks she's a horse; she don't like people."

"Oh. Well, I like horses," I say.

"I'm Delta Hale." The little man holds his hand out to me, in the same way that Mom did to Dixie.

"Why don't you go outside and get to know Dixie while Ayma and I get dinner on the table," Mom tells me.

Mom is halfway down the hall before she turns back to Bud, Delta, and me, who aren't going anywhere. Her bare feet make her look like she could not care less about

Bud or whatever it is about Wren that has kept her in knots. But I know Mom, and I can see her cleavage turning blotchy. Soon the blotches will be all the way up her neck; I'm sticking here with Mom. Bud looks out at the yard toward Dixie.

"Dixie will be fine with Mary Harold, Bud. Let's get these flowers in some water." Mom actually takes Bud by the elbow, leaving me here in the hallway with Delta.

I ignore the boy and go find Dixie; he follows me anyway, same as would an abandoned, mangy dog that needed some fierce fixing up.

In the yard, Delta and I stand around not saying anything to each other but watching Dixie prance.

The whole yard smells like peppermint from when Ayma picked a bunch earlier for the tea. She says the mint keeps taking over the yard, but to me, it's worth keeping just for being able to walk out here and smell it every night. I rub my hands through the mint to keep the smell alive. Delta does the exact same thing. He's already irking me, the way he's following me.

Then he gets all bold. "We're the opposite of you. You ain't got a daddy. Me and Dixie ain't got a mama. She left us to go off to Nashville when I was a baby."

I ignore him some more. He keeps talking like he's the one in charge.

"My sister, Dixie, she ain't right, you know. She thinks she's a horse," Delta tells me.

I don't care one bit for little kids acting like big-shot know-it-alls. I can decide for myself about Dixie.

While Delta starts throwing rocks at the squirrels in Ayma's yard, I watch Dixie. She's not bothering anybody; she's not doing anything, really, except running around in the grass on the last night of June. I'd just call what she's doing pretending.

Dixie circles closer and closer to me, and as she does, I stop watching her directly. I pretend, too. I pretend to ignore her altogether, kind of like how I got to know Sue the day Mom called Bud a cow whisperer. I drop my head and wait for her; I count on her to be curious, just the same as Sue.

When I know Dixie is within earshot, I ask Delta, "So, what kind of horse is your sister?"

Dixie perks up and trots over to us.

Delta rolls his eyes. "Girl, can't you see? She ain't really a horse. She's a girl, like you! She's wack—something's wrong with her."

"Seriously?" I ask, trying to get him riled.

I eyeball Dixie real close. I touch her back; I touch her head; I look her all over.

Dixie is a compact girl, muscular, not skinny. Her

skin is browner than mine, and her hair is long to her waist and jet-black like her little brother's and Bud's.

"Big man, I hate to break it to you, but Dixie is a quarter-horse filly."

Dixie tosses her head repeatedly and neighs.

"See? I'm right. By the way, I'm a draft-Thoroughbred cross."

Dixie leans over and smells me, so I smell her, too.

"You're crazier than her," Delta says. He goes back into the house and lets the screen-porch door slam. I'm happy — now he won't bug us anymore.

I plop down in the grass and look straight ahead. Purposefully, I don't make eye contact with Dixie right away. Staring can make a horse nervous. Being indirect and letting them come to you is more effective, or so I have read.

The night is still too early for lightning bugs just yet; before long they'll be all over this yard. Mom told me once that there are about two thousand different species of this little glowing beetle; they live all over the world. Once the sun sets, they'll start out low to the ground and, as it gets darker, make their way higher and higher until they disappear way above the trees. I keep ignoring Dixie, watching for the first lightning bug.

I weave a clover necklace, carefully avoiding the

bumblebees. Horses are as curious as they are nervous. Sure enough, Dixie sits down beside me. I keep looping the clover blossoms together. Dixie reaches her face out long toward me and her eyes wide and full of white. She blows air out of her nose. I stick my hand out so she sees that I mean no harm. Sure enough, she smells my hand and then makes a rumbling sound. I show Dixie the necklace. I wonder if she is going to try to eat the clover, but she only sniffs at it. I lift the clover necklace over her head and put it around her neck.

"There. Now, you're a pretty, pretty pony," I say, and laugh at my own joke.

I make myself a clover ankle bracelet; my ankle looks dainty. Even my ugly second toe—which is itching like heck out here in the grass—looks right at home. I turn my ankle in circles, admiring my pretty foot.

I look almost girly tonight, with my braided hair and my clover anklet. The old poplars are crazy full of birds getting their fussing out of the way for the night. Their songs jumble up together like one big tangled mess. Mom could pick them all out in a heartbeat if she were out here with us. She'd be sitting right here beside me saying, "Song sparrow. Towhee. Eastern meadowlark. Mocker." I blink the tears out of my eyes and try not to think about Mom leaving tomorrow. I do more ankle circles. Dixie seems pleased with her new clover jewelry and starts to canter around the yard again.

Right this second I feel like I am about a ten, not a three. If Drew Walker, the boy who held me and asked me to dance on a dare, could see me here tonight, stretched out on the grass under these hundred-year-old trees, with that good old, giant moon now full as it can be, beaming across Moulton Valley, he might want to sit right beside me waiting for lightning bugs and crafting jewelry out of clover. Drew Walker doesn't matter anymore, and neither does Krystal or anyone else. Right here, right now, I am taking the first step of making my new life in Wren, Alabama. By the time Mom calls us to dinner, I have made my first real friend in Wren, even if she is a horse.

CHAPTER THIRTEEN

THE DINNER TABLE is fuller than ever—fuller of food and fuller of people. Dixie sits down next to me, smelling every dish that comes our way. Delta sits on my other side, grabbing every dish out of my hands practically before I've even helped myself. I am about ready to smack him.

Except for the oven-fried chicken, biscuits, and the mashed potatoes, every dish has come fresh from Ayma's garden. The season is too early for corn yet, but I could eat just the entire platter of tomatoes for my dinner and nothing else. I pass the squash casserole straight on over to Delta so I can load up on tomatoes and okra. That big bowl full of fried okra has my name, Mary Harold, on it, not his.

Bud's trying to convince Ayma and Mom to get me enrolled in the Indian Education Program at my new school. Dixie and Delta are in it, which makes sense because they're from the Cherokee. Bud's pretty sure nearly everybody from Lawrence County has some Indian blood in them, and so according to Bud, they count as Indian. Bud's like a magical, genealogical expert in tracing people—even red-headed people—back to their Cherokee roots.

Seeing as how Lawrence County was taken from Cherokee lands in the 1800s and how our family lived here even before then, I wonder if the whole county just might be descended from Indians, like Bud seems to think, except for the ones who moved here lately. They could be, too, from some other variety, but someone else would have to find out for them. Even the official county history tells how when the Indians were removed from here by the government and forced to walk to Oklahoma, many vanished into the Black Warrior Forest and lived there. Much later some came back into Lawrence County, passing for white, after having foiled the law by spiriting themselves away to the forest for a good, long while. Of course, the forest was a whole lot bigger then; I guess it took up most of Alabama.

Our dinner table has definitely never been so loud; with Bud's family added, we've doubled from three to six. I can tell by Ayma's stern voice, and how she swats the air around her face when she talks to him, that Bud is plucking her last nerve. "Bud, stop trying to make me an Indian. I'm speaking the truth. Our people were Irish, black Irish. In fact, I've got documentation to prove it," she insists.

Bud won't let it die. "I'm just saying, Miz Woods, Cherokee around here been explaining away their dark hair and dark eyes as black Irish for a couple hundred years now."

Mom starts to speak up, but Ayma interrupts her. "Bud Hale, you know good and well that you have to prove Indian ancestry to get into Indian Education. We're black Irish."

"Okay." He shows both his palms to Ayma like he's in a stickup. Then Bud looks directly at me. "I know I could find you an ancestor."

"Bud!" Mom pipes up in defense of Ayma. "You found her a cow! You are not to find her anything else, got it?"

Bud helps himself to more chicken and biscuits.

Then he asks Mom, "Why don't you hang around awhile, Bye? It'd be nice to catch up."

Mom shakes her head to herself and swallows good before answering real quiet and almost to herself, "I have to get back to work. I'm leaving in the morning." Her voice cracks a little bit. I'm thinking that maybe she has remembered she'll be driving back alone for the first time ever.

Bud drops his head and then cuts his eyes back at Mom. "You hear they're getting ready to hire a new ranger? I head up the citizen board, you know. The forest service could use a woman to help take care of the Black Warrior."

I suppose because she's easily offended, Mom gets all indignant with him, "What the hell does that mean, Bud?"

Ayma pretends that she did not just hear Mom swear at the dinner table by passing the butter, which has already been around twice.

"I don't know." Bud shrugs. "A woman might be better at protecting the forest while there's still something there to be protected. You sure would be. You love that forest more than anyone I know. All those times we canoed down the Sipsey, and hiked to the Big Tree? What do you call the Big Tree? Something to do with wisdom. You still naming every tree you love, Bye?"

Mom turns scarlet again. "Sophia. I call the Big Tree Sophia. It comes from the Greek word for wisdom, Bud."

She looks embarrassed. Delta doesn't pay her any mind; he's stuffing his mouth full of mashed potatoes. Dixie fiddles with her clover necklace. Ayma and I already know how weird she is, so I figure, who cares?

Bud keeps talking to her with his mouth full. "I always loved that about you, that you name your favorite trees. Woman, you are something when you get out there in the woods. I can't believe you ever left us, you know, left Wren. I'd trust you in the forest more than any of my hunting buddies. Hey, remember that time we came upon a hermit and he liked to scared us to death?" Bud asks Mom.

Mom has frozen stiff as a three-day-old dead cat found in a hot shed. She is not moving. She is mortified, I can tell, at the easy way Bud is bringing all this up.

Good old oblivious Bud looks amazed at this memory. He turns to Ayma. "Man, that was a lifetime ago." Then he stares across the table at us, like all of a sudden he remembers we're here, too.

"None of y'all were born yet. Mary Harold"—Bud points his finger like a gun at me— "I guess this would've been about a year or so before you were born. Right, Bye? You'd come back from Virginia for a visit."

Mom is blotchy all up and down her chest and neck. The confidence that dress was giving her earlier has gone on down Wren Mountain. Everybody else has perked up to hear the story, though, so Bud keeps on telling it.

"I mean, we were deep in the forest. We thought we were all alone, not a soul around. I reckon we were several miles off the trail. This old guy—real wild and unkempt, looking about exactly the way you'd expect a hermit to look, with this crazy red beard, no shirt, and wearing green pants that were not by any means new—just came up from out of the wilderness. Startled the bejesus out of me. Bye, of course, acted like he was twenty minutes late for a noon reservation. Fella stood there looking at us full-on for about ten seconds, then took off running like the law was after him. Bye wanted to chase after him, see if she could get him to talk to us. She wanted him to tell us everything we didn't know about the forest. I'm not imagining that, am I, Bye?"

Mom opens her balled-up fist. She looks right into Bud's face and smiles; I guess she remembers Bud and the forest, too. For the first time, she looks directly at him and puts her hand on top of his. "No, Bud, you're not imagining the hermit. We saw him. We surely did."

By the look on her face, it must have been a real nice day.

The rest of us are quiet now and looking at anything but Mom and Bud. I watch the ceiling. I'm partial to staring at Ayma's crown molding because it really is exactly the same in every room in the house. But a sort of glowing bubble has sprung up around Mom and Bud, and the crown molding just doesn't have the same magnetic effect. I try keeping one eye on the crown molding and one eye on the two of them, but my eyes hurt straight off doing that.

Then, while Mom is still resting her hand on top of his, Bud tells her, "Maybe you belong in Wren with your daughter, Bye. Ever thought of that?"

Bud sets his fork down on his plate and then just looks at Mom plain in the face. She's real beety now on every visible inch of herself.

These past few days, Mom has complained about Bud, made faces at Bud, and even tried to get Ayma to fire Bud. Mom acts like she can't stand the fact that Bud takes care of Ayma's cows, her land, and her house when something goes wrong. But Mom has hardly taken her eyes off Bud since we got here. My shy mom must think she's invisible. I, for one, have seen her checking him out. Bud knows it, too; maybe that's why he's asking her to stay. Maybe her voice is cracking because she knows everybody at this table, except probably the bratty Delta, knows the truth: *Mom still likes Bud.*

Ayma excuses herself and orders us kids with her: "Come on, young'uns, help me get these dishes up. Then we'll have our cake and ice cream."

Dixie, Delta, and I clear all the plates in one trip.

Ayma has made my favorites—a coconut cake and homemade peach ice cream. I let Dixie bring my birthday cake to the table; I carry the birthday flowers and Delta the ice cream. A lime-green spider crawls around my flowers. I keep a little scream inside of me and hand the flowers to Mom again.

Fourteen blue candles are lit atop my coconut cake, one for each year of my life and one to grow on. Every year I wonder what it means to light a candle to grow on. Maybe it means all of the growing mistakes of this year will get burned away.

Everybody except for Dixie sings to me; even Delta sings. I blow out the candles and make one long birthday wish that I keep to myself. Mom and Ayma both hand me presents; I open Ayma's first. I get a pair of knitting needles, even though I don't knit. "Thank you, Ayma," I say, and mean it. "I've been wanting to learn to knit for a while now."

"Well, good. I'd be glad to teach you."

Then I shake an unwrapped red box from Mom.

Inside, she has strung a white seashell on a silver chain. I recognize this shell and remember finding it at Oak Island last summer.

"Oh, Mom." I get up to hug her.

"You'll always know I'm with you, right, Cricket?"

Dixie shakes her head and blows air out of her nose when she hears Mom call me Cricket. Like me, Mom is not allowing herself to be spooked by Dixie's "different way of communicating."

She tells Dixie, "*Cricket* is my special name for Mary Harold. She loved to catch crickets in her hands when she was a little girl. Something went awry, though, didn't it? She wouldn't touch a cricket today if you paid her."

I nod. "That's totally true." Then I tell Dixie, "I'll still hold lightning bugs, though."

Bud tells me, "You'll have another present before too long. I suspect Sue is going to go anytime now. Speaking of which, I'm hoping we can fix some of these fences before we add any more calves. You feel like helping me out tomorrow?"

"Sure."

"Good. Good. You can be my summer helper—how about that?"

"Okay. Maybe I can help all year."

Dixie and Delta start kicking each other under the table. Dixie is whinnying up a storm.

"Come on, Dixie," I say. "Let's go catch lightning bugs."

All around us, the Black Warrior Forest has closed up Wren Mountain for the night. The sky is dark enough that the lightning bugs are easy to see now and still low enough to catch in our hands. Dixie doesn't try to catch them but leaves that to me. Delta captures them one by one and tears their tails off for the fun of it, then presses them onto his fingers. I have the urge to punch this boy I just met to make him stop killing my favorite bug. He's not my brother; heck, I hardly know this kid, but he is not making himself a new friend tonight.

"You're his big sister. Can't you make him stop?" I ask Dixie.

She canters away from me like she didn't hear a word. When I tell that boy to cut it out, he laughs and keeps pulling off tails until all his fingers are lit up.

"Hey!" I holler at him. "Don't do that!"

"They're just stupid fireflies; they can't feel it." He ignores me and doubles up on some of his fingers.

"Stop it, I said! No killing lightning bugs in my yard!"

His ignoring me ticks me off so bad that, without really thinking, I pop him hard on the head.

"Ow!" Delta rubs his head like I really hurt him. "This ain't your yard. This is Miz Woods' yard. I'm tellin'!"

I almost shove him, but I don't because he's little and because I'm not the shoving type and that pop just fired out of my hand by surprise. But I have to let him know I mean business about the no killing rule.

"Go ahead and tell. See if I care," I say, and hope he won't.

Delta slinks off to the screen porch and watches Dixie and me from Ayma's rocking chair. He sits there in the dark, rocking in that chair like crazy. I ignore him this time. I know he's watching us, and I'm glad he's run off to pout. I go back to catching lightning bugs for Dixie and me.

I'm more into catch and release; I don't even use a pickle jar. Gently, I hold the fireflies in my hands, but only for a minute. When finally thirteen lightning bugs inside my closed palms all fire their tails at once, my hands light up the night like a lantern. I call Dixie over quickly.

"Dixie! Come make a wish on my birthday lights."

She trots to me, then stomps her foot.

I hold my cupped hands near her mouth. "Here, make a wish, then we'll set them free."

With my back to Moulton Valley, I stand facing the

Black Warrior Forest and open my hands. Dixie blows gently across my palms. By turns, all the fireflies flash and fire up toward the poplars. Except for Delta rocking that rocker like he's trying to take off, I ask for more nights just exactly like this one. I wonder if Dixie asks for the same.

CHAPTER FOURTEEN

ON SUNDAY MORNING, I find Mom reading the paper at the kitchen table. Tomatoes are piled up on the sink; I can tell Ayma must be up and about, too. She's probably working in the garden. Mom has showered and dressed; she is ready to drive back. I wish for her to tell me that everything will be fine and that she will stay on Wren Mountain with us.

"Hi," she sings like today's a normal day.

"Hi, Mom. I love you." I go sit in her lap. My weight and my height must be uncomfortable for her. But I need to be wrapped up in her one more time before she goes away. I rest my head on her shoulder and shut my eyes in her neck. She smells like cinnamon.

"Did you eat cinnamon toast?" I ask without needing to ask.

"I did." She kisses my forehead. "Want some? I'll make it for you."

I nod but keep her tied to her chair and to me.

Mom wraps both her arms around me tight. "Don't worry," she whispers. "You're going to be fine. I think you're right. Wren is where you need to be right now."

"Maybe Wren is where you need to be, too," I plead with her, "like Bud said."

Mom brushes my hair out of my eyes. "I don't know."

"But maybe it could be, Mom. If there actually is a job in the Black Warrior and if I'm here, and anyway, you're a grown-up now. Maybe everything would be different."

"Could be," she says. "You could be right."

"Really?"

"Well, it's obvious to me that being up here on this hill and being up here with your cow has already given you confidence. In just these few days, you seem more at ease. I mean, not once have you had a panic attack. I have some hard questions to face when I get home."

She is right; I feel different. I rest my head on Mom again and think of nothing. I want a few empty minutes of holding my mom without anything good or bad in my mind.

"Cricket," Mom says, "this is your chance to be yourself. You get a new start; whatever or whoever you are to become is all up to you. School starts in six weeks. Don't be afraid to stick up for yourself if you need to. And will ya keep an eye on Dixie? Ayma says Dixie has it tough at school. You might watch out for her."

"Okay," I promise. I lower my voice and ask, "What do you think is wrong with Dixie?"

I hear the porch door slam; Ayma's in from weeding.

"Morning, Glory." She kisses me. "Now, girls, what's wrong with who?"

"Ayma? Why is Dixie that way? And why is Delta his way?"

She pulls up a chair between Mom and me; I can tell she is settling in for a serious explanation. She sighs. "My beauty, there's a certain strain of peculiar in that family, and it kindy flared up when Starlett left for Nashville."

Ayma is not gossiping; she speaks without a whisper or lowered head. She is sharing facts.

"Starlett is Dixie's mom?" I ask.

"Right, Starlett is Dixie's mom. Delta's too, of course."

When Starlett's name comes up, Mom fidgets me to her other knee. "Mother, could we not talk about Starlett? Let's not go there."

I stand up, out of Mom's lap, and try to touch the

ceiling. "Ouch, Mom," I tease her. "Okay, who really cares about this Starlett, anyway? I just want to know what it means to have a 'certain strain of peculiar.' Do I have one?"

Ayma explains, "Well, peculiar means different things in different people. Sometimes there can be a tendency to turn into a bit of an unusual person under the correct circumstances."

Then, all-knowingly, Ayma turns to Mom. "Both Bud's children get all kinds of special services from the county. I don't know the exact trouble, what it's called exactly, but I know Bud struggles mightily, raising them on his own. He's a good man, Bye. He does right by those children. And for your information, I wasn't intending on saying anything more about Starlett. I don't know a thing more than what's been said, anyway. She's been gone from Wren forever, and I don't expect she's coming back. Starlett's done more than her fair share of damage to Bud and those children."

I wonder if that Starlett gave Dixie the strain of peculiar. Mom doesn't struggle mightily with me. Maybe Dixie and Delta got their strain from their daddy.

Without thinking, I blurt out, "Delta pulled the tails off of those lightning bugs like that's a normal, okay thing to do. I don't even know my father, but I didn't turn into a horse or an evil boy in a plaid shirt." I leave out the part about me smacking Delta on the head.

I slide into the chair beside Ayma. Ayma looks hard at me, as if she is sizing me up for the first time ever.

"No, you turned into something else entirely," Ayma says. Then she adds, "We all have our burdens to carry, Mary Harold. If I didn't know you like I do, your recent actions could be cast in a very different light, couldn't they?"

"What do you mean?" I ask. I feel a little blood flushing my face.

Mom has a sort of sad smile. She shakes her head and then gives me some advice. "Here we go, Cricket. You might as well learn. Try not to look directly into her eyes, sweetie—that only makes it worse."

In a calm way that doesn't sound like I'm in trouble but makes me feel like I was wrong to judge Dixie and Delta, Ayma brings me to a different way of seeing my own peculiar self. "Well, you showed up on my doorstep after stealing your mother's truck, her credit card, and driving clear across tarnation at thirteen years old. You could have wrecked the truck, been arrested, killed, carjacked, kidnapped—"

"Mother, stop it. You're making your point," Mom interrupts.

"At the very least," Ayma asks, drilling right into me with those blue eyes that Mom says are the sweetest blue of the cerulean warbler, "could we not all agree that your behavior might be considered peculiar? I mean, of course, if we didn't fully understand all the circumstances and history leading up to your arrival here."

I hang my head and nod.

Ayma caresses my chin and lifts my face up to hers. I am trapped. Her eyes are the only place I want to be anyhow. "What we hope for," my grandmother almost whispers, "and have to believe, is that God will give us the strength we need to get through our life just fine."

She pauses. "More than fine. You're gon' be more than fine."

We're all three quiet, not knowing exactly who should say what next. I halfway think that if nobody talks, then Mom won't leave.

I trace the wood grain in the kitchen table over and over. The kitchen table is about as old as this house and made from Black Warrior yellow poplar trees, the same kind of trees that line the drive. Ayma told me once that her great-great-great-granddaddy made this table in 1837 after a terrible storm tore through Lawrence County. Poplar grain is real irregular in color; there's one panel of wood in the table where the grain runs along the board almost exactly the way Wren Mountain runs along the horizon if you're looking up from Moulton Valley about the time the sun sets.

I remember this table way back from forever ago, when I was little. Ayma's yard was full of clover flowers—clover flowers and bumblebees. Bumblebees, real yellow-and-black ones, look powdery soft. I had put my foot out to feel the bee's powdery softness, and all I remember next is Ayma holding me on this exact table, singing to me on this exact table, and distracting me from something both screaming hot and soothing cold on my foot.

Mom never remembers this happening. While I have Ayma and Mom here with me, I ask, "Did I sit on this table after a bumblebee sting?"

Ayma remembers right away. "You surely did, beauty. You were a little thing about eighteen months old. You stepped right on a big, fat bumblebee and cried those big ol' sorry tears, tears so big they made me and your mother cry right along with you."

"Mom was here?"

"Yes, she was. Bye doctored you up. I sat on the table and held you in my arms. We sang nursery rhymes, and Bye rubbed your foot with witch hazel. That's the way we did it back then, with witch hazel. Then I took you to the front porch and rocked you over the valley till you fell asleep."

"I remember that now," Mom says more to herself than to Ayma or me.

So Mom took care of me; they both took care of me. In a few minutes, my life will be different. Mom will go.

"Cutie, do you still want that cinnamon toast?" Mom asks.

I perk up. "Yes, please. Could you make it with lots of butter and extra cinnamon?"

But I don't have to tell her; Mom is the only one who has ever made cinnamon toast for me. I guess she is taking care of me now even in our very last minute together.

CHAPTER FIFTEEN

AYMA AND I STAND ON THE ROAD waving until Mom's hybrid car looks like a tin bug in the distance, then we keep on waving until all of the dust is back at rest. For a minute, after she's gone on, I wonder if I made it all up. What if my life wasn't so bad? What if things would have been better?

I start to take off down the mountain after Mom, but my Adam's apple swells up, blocking the air from getting to my lungs, causing my heart to pound loud in my ears. I feel achy in my temples, too.

Ayma slips her arm around my waist and pulls me back toward the house. "I have a feeling we'll see her back here before you know it."

"Really?"

"You never know. You never know what might be churning inside that gal, my dear. I wouldn't, in a month of Sundays, have expected to have you all to myself. But I do."

I hold Ayma and I kiss the top of her head. Her hair is mostly white now, with a few strands of brown left underneath.

Neither of us goes inside for a while. Ayma waters the purple coneflowers and leaves the dead heads for the birds. She pays special attention to watering her prized hosta. "Hummingbirds sure do love this hosta," Ayma mumbles to herself.

Mom's right, I decide. Here I can be whoever I want to be. "Aren't you supposed to run go help Bud this morning?" Ayma reminds me.

"Yep. I just have one thing to do first."

I race upstairs to my room, my new room, which I love more than I have loved any other room. It will only hold Ayma's old cherry bed with its canopy, matching bureau, and dressing table; it's small, but perfect for me. Ayma keeps her sewing in the dressing table, but I don't mind sharing the space. My two windows give me plenty of light. I love the way the lace curtains fly around when I bring in the wind. From the window by my bed, I can see all of Moulton Valley, almost all the way to Decatur.

All alone, looking across the valley, I unbraid my hair and let it fall down past my shoulders. I braid my hair back again, this time in a French braid. I've been braiding my hair by myself since fourth grade. Ayma taught me how; that's how she wears her hair. Ayma's hair is way longer than mine.

In front of the mirror at the dressing table, I pretend that I have never seen me. Here and now, I decide who I am. I will be a girl who speaks up for herself; no longer will I be silent like I was in Virginia. I always hid in my hair and held on to my hair, hoping for something to change. But now I decide. I have Dixie, I have Sue, and most of all, I have Ayma. For today, I have everything I need to know who I am in Wren.

Ayma keeps her sewing scissors sharp and in the top drawer of the dressing table. I cut the braid off at my shoulder, and it is still too long, so I cut to my chin and I give myself bangs, then I cut to my ears. I keep cutting until there's only an inch or two of hair left all the way around my head. Waiting there under all of my hair, what I see now in the mirror is definitely something new.

I have a cameo neck, one of those long, swan ones. I mean, I look like a modern sort of cameo, with really short hair. I look beautiful. Especially beautiful, too, are my ears; I might go to Decatur and get them pierced one of these days. I'm not gross or disgusting at all. I am new.

When I hear Ayma coming up the stairs, I start to hide her scissors but change my mind, because it's my hair and I wanted it off.

"Ayma," I call out, "come here."

She steps into the doorway, and before she can catch herself, she gasps. "Lord, baby!" Hair coats my shoulders, hides my lap, and covers the floor.

"Well," I start explaining, "I was only planning on cutting a little bit, but I got carried away."

Ayma giggles. "I'll say."

I fluff my bangs up and pull the sideburn thingies down to make them look even.

"What do you think?" I ask.

"Stay right there," she tells me. "I'll be back in a jiff."

Ayma comes back with a towel and a razor. "Let's polish you up just a tad," she suggests. "I'm an old pro, you know. I used to cut your grandfather's hair and shave him every few weeks. He loved for me to do that for him. We'd make a big production of it. I'd set us up in the front yard, heat up a tub of water, and we'd take our time under the shade trees — talking and cutting his hair, shaving his neck and face. Well, that was our special time, believe it or not."

She shaves the back of my neck and then evens up my bangs and the sides. Now I look really gorgeous. I look like I'm from New York. Even better, I'm from Wren.

I get up to leave, but Ayma calls me back. "Hold on. You have to do me now. I've been thinking about going short for twenty-some years." This is Ayma's way of sticking with me, I think.

My hands tremble a little at first, but then Ayma winks at me, and I know she'll fix it herself if I mess up. I cut Ayma's braid, just like I did mine. I cut to her shoulders and then to her chin. I am afraid to keep chopping, so I hand Ayma the scissors. She gives herself the same haircut as mine.

"I'll clean all this up," Ayma tells me with a kiss. "You get over to Bud's." When I look back, I catch Ayma admiring herself in the mirror. "I look right pretty. Now, shoo!"

I race across the field to Bud's. My new hair feels good in the sunshine.

Bud's place backs up to the Black Warrior Forest, same as ours. His heifer field and ours are right alongside each other, and we've got gates in between so the fields can be shared. The field is still damp from the morning dew, and my boots look like they have been painted with perfect teardrops of yellow from walking through all the buttercups.

There's a hole in the front fence on the other side of the road. The cows haven't gotten out yet, but Bud says the first thing Sue will do when we bring her over with the rest of the herd is to look for a way out because each new one acts up at first. We get a later start mending the fence line than we had planned. For now, we patch the hole with scrap wood.

I hold the plank tight to the fence post while Bud hammers. My hands turn pink, then red, then white, and then my arms start shaking until I feel a bruise growing on my wrists and my body just quits on me, but I make myself hold the board for Bud until he nods at me, which I can tell means it's okay for me to go ahead and take a break.

I am going to need to get stronger.

Bud picks up the hammer again. This time, I try holding the board by leaning my hips and my whole body weight against the plank. My legs absorb the pounding. Thankfully, Bud doesn't comment on what a weakling I am. All he says is, "Thanks," when we're done with the first plank. He also tells me, "I like your haircut."

Working so hard out here, I am loving my new haircut. Sweat is trickling through my bangs, behind my ears, and actually cooling me off instead of matting my long hair to my neck like it would have done.

We must walk five or ten miles over the course of the morning. We walk the fence in every field—back and forth across Ayma's six hundred acres and what feels like the same for Bud's land—fixing boards, cutting sharp wires, and making notes of what we'll need to do next time. By the end of the day, Bud seems ready to start all over and I just want to collapse. The new me has a new haircut and another new friend; now I need some new muscles, too.

Chapter Sixteen

ON MY FIRST NIGHT WITHOUT MOM, while she is driving back to Virginia without me and I am sleeping on Wren Mountain, I dream of a forest thick enough to disappear into forever and so full that its waterfalls roar or whisper within earshot of every step. This place is thick and wild. I am uncomfortable to go farther, yet I'm unable to turn back, for behind me there is nothing but blackness. I am not in an African jungle; the world before me is more like an American jungle, because this is forest life that I recognize, just too much of it: pine, oak, cedar, poplar, redbud, and a carpet of fern and moss rolling toward my feet so quickly that I cannot turn away. There is no discernible trail to follow, only years of fallen leaves on the forest floor.

I search the tree trunks for blazes, like the ones Mom paints on the trees in the Pocahontas Forest to mark the trails for hikers. But there are no blue, white, or red blazes to guide me. And this is not the Pocahontas Forest. This is the Black Warrior Forest, the forest that called Mom to serve, the same way some people are called by God to preach.

This forest is too wild for me. Mom's not afraid, though; she knows all the right places to go to find waterfalls and swimming holes. She knows which trees the Indians bent centuries ago to mark their turns and intersections. My mom could walk to Sophia, her big tree, with a scarf hiding her face.

I look around for Mom; she'll know where I am.

I call out her proper name: "Tabythia? Tabythia Woods."

There is no answer, no human sound. I hear every other voice in the forest, except Mom's.

"Tabythia, please, come out," I shout up into the thick canopy. I spin around, hoping that the rustle behind me is Mom.

Standing before me is a plain Indian girl who looks

about my age. She isn't a fancy dancer like you some-times see at powwows. She isn't dressed modern like most of the Indians that Mom knows from her work. The girl wears a sandy-colored tunic that's up to her thighs. She is strong and muscular like I want to become. The shadows and light in my dream reveal defined strength in her arms and legs. There are no feathers in her hair or beadwork on her dress. Around her neck, she wears a long deer-bead necklace, like the ones I've seen at the museum. But this girl is not extinct.

She looks directly into the well of me, like she knows what-all is in there. She understands that sometimes I can't breathe at all. She knows my fear of dying, and I know she saw me smack Delta. I feel ashamed and wish I could take it back.

When I try to explain, she turns and runs off.

I run right through all the forest underbrush without fear of branches catching my eye or poison ivy brushing my legs. I chase her.

"Wait," I call. I am afraid without her. Alone in this forest, I am scared even to stand still. The deeper we go, the thicker the forest canopy is, and so the darker the forest gets. The darkness scares me.

In her bare feet the girl runs so fast that, sprinting at my top speed, I nearly lose her. Abruptly, she stops at an ancient tree with bark unidentifiable to me at first, with so much of its base protected by a thick coverlet of moss. I peel the soft, damp moss away from the tree while the girl watches. The straight ridges of the bark are so deep that I can tuck my fingers in between them. This old tree is a yellow poplar—Mom's favorite.

The girl points up. The poplar's branches unfold into a house that extends beyond the canopy of the forest, beyond the highest cumulus cloud, and even beyond the farthest blue space of my eye. The rooftop must surely reach all the way to God, for this is Sophia, the Big Tree. Mom stands on the balcony, waving at me to come up. I take one single step toward her, and the earth convulses so violently that the Big Tree shakes, too, and begins to fall. I watch Mom tumble easily, from limb to limb, until she is standing next to me.

I don't try to explain the girl to Mom because I am too busy mourning Sophia. Mom does not cry for the loss, but I do. Mom tells me, "Don't be afraid, Cricket."

I turn to the girl and ask, "Who are you?"

She takes off running into the forest again. This time, I know to follow her. Like before, my breath is shallow and painful. The girl stops behind our barn.

I feel faint from the hard running and bend over to steady my breathing. The air burns my lungs; I close my eyes and try to resist taking breaths. I take short, shallow breaths until finally the pain eases enough for me to find oxygen. The girl breathes easily and without effort.

She waits for me to recover, then urges me to come closer. A newborn deer rests at her feet. The girl kneels down, then looks up at me as she did before. She speaks one word: *Awanita*. She motions for me to pick up the deer. He is covered in blood and wet from birth. Again, she urges me to pick him up. I am afraid of the forest and afraid of what she is asking me to do. I run away.

I wake up sweating and short of breath. My head hurts, too. Ayma has turned off the air-conditioning again. My room is sweltering. I open both windows in my room and turn on the ceiling fan to pull in the cooler night air. The cows are quiet up here on Wren Mountain. Looking out across the valley, I can see lights from Decatur along Highway 72. I see the moon, too. Some people might be watching the sky thinking they are sitting under a full moon, but they're not. The moon is missing a tiny slice of itself tonight.

Mom might be all the way back to Virginia by now.

Chapter Seventeen

THE WAY BUD'S TRUCK COMES TEARING across the road means something is wrong in the field. Sue's been ready for almost two weeks, since we both first got to Wren. I feel it; now is her time. I look toward the back pasture, where Sue is, and see two turkey vultures starting to circle. I tell myself that doesn't mean a thing. Those birds would circle our house if Ayma started coughing in December.

"Mary Harold! Sue's about ready to give up—she needs you," Bud yells from his truck. He doesn't even cut the engine or get out.

"Come on," he repeats. "Sue needs you." He doesn't say, "She needs us" or "She needs help." Bud says, "She needs you."

Without him having to explain, I know Sue is having a difficult birth. We have all been waiting for Sue to go, and I have counted every one of the last fourteen days. Sue is overdue. Before I can get halfway in the truck, Bud is backing down the drive.

In the field, neither of us bothers to shut the truck doors. When we get to her, Sue is still and quiet, but breathing too hard. She can barely keep her eyes open.

I wonder if she just fell down here, maybe in pain, and could not get back up, because she is laboring in full sun, in the middle of the field. No other cows are around her; all of them are standing at the back fence under the shade of the trees. That sort of makes me think something must have gone wrong and Sue couldn't make it to a safe, comfortable place. Could be that she was on her way to the three cedars in the corner. Possibly she was on her way nowhere and the pain came because her calf insisted on coming now. Maybe he got stuck and had no choice but to lay his mother down to labor in the sun.

I think Sue might be dying. I am here for her. Her baby is halfway out and not moving at all. What I see of it is all black, like Sue. I can't see the calf's head, only its back legs. Flies are everywhere on what's sticking out of the calf, and flies are all over Sue, too.

"If we work fast, we might save them both," says Bud. I am having a heart attack, I think. A sharp pain under my ribs jabs too deep at my heart, so I cut my breath short and just stop inhaling, hoping something will change inside me now.

"Champ? You okay?"

Sue's eyes are closed. I hear Bud calling me, and I am looking for one good breath for myself and for Sue. Breathing is too hard; I might die here with Sue.

Sue opens her brown eyes. My mom has those eyes; I didn't forget them. I am not afraid, I decide. I am not having a heart attack; I'm only thirteen.

I make my short-haired self breathe in deep, and the pain in my chest is still there, bigger than all get-out, and I do want to stop breathing, but I don't until it's time to breathe out. So I do, long and slow. Sue's eyes are open. I breathe.

"I'm okay, Bud."

"Good girl! That's my girl! Keep doing what you're doing. This calf's got to get some air or we're finished."

"I don't understand what's wrong. You said Sue had calved before. Why is the baby stuck?"

"This calf is too big; Sue must have bred to a big bull.

This is just too much for her. She can't do it alone." He hides his face in the crook of his arm, just for a second. "And it's a breech, which isn't doing us any favors."

I wonder if Bud is giving up, too.

We can't give up yet; I won't give up on Sue. I sit down beside Bud and wrap both my hands around the calf's back hock. Bud nods at me. He holds the left one and says, "On three." Then he counts, "One. Two. Three." We pull to our maximum, then rest.

"Again. One, two, three," counts Bud. We pull hard until Bud says, "Okay," meaning stop for a minute.

I hear a car come tearing down our road at lightning speed, in too much of a hurry. So few people live on this road that we don't get speeders often. Sue startles a little and tries to get up. We help her settle, and then we pull again until Bud and I are nearly laid out straight, flat on our backs.

"Let's try it one more time," Bud says to me.

Once more, we hold the calf and pull, together. A steady stream of sweat runs down the middle of my back. I am not going to stop.

Poor old Sue; she starts crying, and it doesn't take any special listening skills to see that she is getting wore out and losing hope. I believe I see a little more of the calf's body; I can't be sure. Bud looks directly at me, then at Sue. She is having trouble keeping her eyes open. She is bleeding because all our pulling is tearing her. Turkey vultures seem to be coming from nowhere. I want to scream at them or throw rocks at the sky. Even though I don't want her to see all the buzzards, she needs to keep her eyes open for me. I whisper to Sue, "Don't close your eyes, girl. You're gonna be okay."

"Mary Harold," Bud tells me, "go on up there and talk to her some. I think I can work this end."

Sue seems relieved to have me sit with her. She knew it was me all along, but she rests her head against my leg when she hears my voice in her ear. I figure the least I can do is keep the flies out of her eyes. I gently brush them away and blow on her face to cool her off. Every few minutes, Sue cries, and I wish I could make it stop for her. When Bud pulls, Sue pushes her big head into me. I am glad to take some of the weight for her. We work real hard together, all three of us, trying to save that calf. Sometimes, though, I guess you do have to give up.

When I helped my first calf get born with Bud the other day, I got grossed out completely—grossed out enough to throw up behind a round bale. I threw up until I couldn't get anything else up and was only heaving emptiness. My hands were covered in blood and guts that stayed on me, forming a crust that looked like a thick layer of mud, all dried and cracked. Afterward, I scrubbed my hands hard until they were blistered and torn from my hard scrubbing. Ayma smeared lotion all over my hands and made me cover them with socks during the night.

This time, though, when it's Sue's calf, the blood doesn't bother me. I hardly notice. Sue's crying sure bothers me. After a while, she won't stop, and it doesn't sound like a moo. Her crying starts sounding more like, *NOOOhhh. NOOOhhh,* like a long, drawn-out plea for all this to just stop.

I do not freak out or panic while Sue is losing her calf. I stay right by Sue's head, talking to her like I do every day, saying the same things that I say when I visit her in the field, in the same voice I use every day. I want Sue to hear something familiar. I want her to feel comforted by the things she knows — the way Ayma's starting a load of laundry after I'm in bed comforts me.

I just make my sounds. *Hey, girl, how ya doing? Look at that cloud up there, the one that looks like a genie bottle. Good girl, what a good girl.* Over and over I make those sounds. Together, Bud and I assist Sue through pretty near an hour of labor; we don't stop until way after we should have quit. Who knows how long she had been laboring without us?

After such a hard time, it's common for the mama cow to give up, according to Bud. For all we try, we cannot get Sue's baby out alive. The calf, a little bull, is stillborn. Had that calf come out headfirst like usual, all of us might have walked away nothing more than tired. Had Sue's baby been a tiny bit smaller, we'd have found him nursing instead of dying. And we wouldn't have seen one buzzard waiting.

Once we get the calf all the way out of her, Sue stops crying. I look up at Bud and demand that he tell me what happened. "Why couldn't we save him? Why didn't you come get me earlier? We could have saved him!"

Bud stands over Sue and me, looking at us like he wishes he could start the day over. He doesn't even seem to mind that his orange work pants are all brown now from dirt and Sue's dried blood.

He takes off his cap and rubs his sweaty hair before telling me, "Mary Harold, it's called acceptance. Sometimes, we have to accept what has happened and not look for a tidy explanation and not wish to change things. If we do that, then we allow grace to take over. Letting go is not the same thing as giving up, you know."

When he says that, Sue raises her head up and looks directly at Bud. He tells her, "You were heroic, Sue." She rumbles low, then drops her head back into my lap.

CHAPTER EIGHTEEN

MY GRIEF FOR SUE'S LITTLE BULL gets cut short because there is work still to be done. Bud and I decide to drag the calf into the woods at the back field. I run across the road to Ayma's barn to find a rope. I run so fast and hard that my lungs are pierced with a pain that cuts off every breath I need and raising my hands above my head doesn't help.

I grab hold of the tractor tire to steady myself from the heat, or maybe from the rushing feeling of knowing what I will find behind the barn. Even before it changes, I know the wind will stir itself up and it will feel cool on my face. When that sweet breeze does comes off of

Wren Mountain, I am ready and I am grateful. I breathe it in. I walk to the barn, already believing and ready to not believe, too. Before me, resting in a circle of matted-down grass, lies the newborn fawn of my dream.

I know enough about deer to know that mama deer will often hide their babies while they go off foraging. This baby is still wet from birth.

In my dream, I ran away from the deer. But today is real. I look around to be certain Delta is nowhere nearby; I don't see him. I wish I did see Dixie. Then, like I know I am supposed to do, I lift the deer close to my chest and carry him back to the field.

He is warm and quiet and bloody. The baby sticks to my arms and neck; he starts to shake. By the time I get back to Sue, Bud has dragged her dead son off into the woods on his own and delivered the afterbirth. Sue, still collapsed, hasn't moved at all.

"I don't need the rope. I went on and—" Bud looks up and sees the fawn and me. "I'll be Johnny, girl," he whispers. I kneel beside him, still cradling the newborn.

Our eyes lock, and I want to tell Bud so much about this deer, about what I know and what I think I know. He looks around the pasture and even beyond the field. Then Bud just says, "Okay, champ, we've lost one today. I reckon we're not losing another." Bud stays beside me, showing me what to do. I rub Sue's afterbirth on the fawn until he is covered with her birthing smell. Then I tuck him into Sue's curve; we wait.

Bud wipes his sweat and Sue's blood from his face with a bandana. He hands over his dirty bandana to me.

Right away, Sue licks the baby deer clean, and he begins searching for her milk. Bud smiles at me and says, "That's good, Mary Harold, that you listened."

"Listened to what?" No way Bud knows I dreamed up this baby deer way before I found him.

Bud turns away from Wren and stands facing the Black Warrior Forest. He closes his eyes and extends both arms out to the dark tree line behind the field. "Well, you must have asked the forest for something, and the forest has sent you a message," Bud tells me.

I wipe my face with Bud's blue-and-white bandana. It's full of holes and every bit as soft as the sheets on my bed, sheets that Ayma has probably been washing for fifty years. I wonder how many stillborn calves Bud has delivered in his life. I hand the bandana back to him.

"What's the message?" The forest and the deer are still. The baby doesn't shake anymore, not from fear or from loneliness or from cold. Watching the newborn with my cow, I feel still now, too.

"You tell me, champ. What does the deer mean to you?"

"I never really thought about deer till now. Deer are gentle, I guess."

"True enough." Bud takes off his cap again and looks over at the deer resting with Sue. "Don't be fooled, though—deer are also very powerful."

"Huh. I could see that," I say, but I am only being polite because I really think deer are mostly gentle and quiet, and I am feeling that way now, having been so close to this baby—gentle and quiet.

Then Bud adds, "Cricket, deer know what most people don't: the power of gentleness is often stronger than the power of brute force."

I nod a little like I agree with Bud, even though he might as well be speaking in tongues like they do at that church down the road that used to be a convenience store.

We hop in Bud's truck to ride home to get cleaned up. I think of something else about deer, how they always seem to live together in herds and what if that's the message the forest brought me today. Maybe this deer is the forest's way of telling me that I will find my place of belonging on Wren Mountain or that me being here with Ayma is just like Sue taking on this baby: it's not exactly a perfect fit the way you might expect, but it's a perfect fit for the situation. Even if I'm wrong, I pretend I'm right, but I keep this message all for myself and don't speak it out loud to Bud.

"What if the fawn's mama comes back to the barn looking for him? He'll be attached to Sue."

Bud doesn't hear me. He's distracted by what looks like a hoof, sticking out from the Queen Anne's lace on the roadside. Bud pulls the truck off to the shoulder and we get out. The carcass is a doe; her own afterbirth is resting in her hind legs. The flies swarm the afterbirth like it's Christmas; I feel queasy.

Something must have startled the doe away from the barn right after she gave birth. We go on and pull her all the way into the ditch.

"This is a pretty fresh hit, huh? Rigor mortis hasn't even started," Bud says while jiggling the doe's legs around with ease. "I'd say here's your answer. That baby deer needed a mama about the same moment that Sue needed a calf."

"Do you think Sue will take to the baby deer?" I ask.

Bud nods. "Oh, yeah. So what'll we name him?" he asks me.

I think back to the girl in the forest. What did she say in my dream?

I remember. "Awanita," I tell Bud. The word is new to me, but it feels right in my mouth. I say it again: "Awanita."

Bud chuckles to himself. "Are you sure y'all aren't Indian?"

"What? What does that mean?"

"*Awanita* is Tsalagi, Cherokee, for baby deer."

We name the baby deer Awanita.

Chapter Nineteen

SINCE MOM TOLD THE HEN PARTY to take care of me, Ayma and her friends have started a knitting circle at our house. On Wednesday nights, instead of going to church, the ladies come over to our house for supper to knit and be a support for each other. Ayma says that knitting circle might as well be church because two or more are gathered, and they're all Baptists, except Ayma, who is Methodist, only on a technicality. You know there's bound to be praying, which there is.

At first, Mom was a big bitch about knitting circle, trying to tell Ayma that this is a violation of Mom's second rule—no church. Ayma just laughed at her.

Now the knitters love Ayma's and my matching haircuts. At first they were totally shocked to see our long locks completely gone, especially Madilee Simms, until Ayma said, "Close your mouth, Madilee. My foot, you've seen short-haired women before. It's a mark of distinction to be able to wear your hair this short, am I right, Cricket?"

I didn't have a second to answer because Bud chimed on in: "You were beauties before, and now both y'all are more striking than ever, Miz Woods, and that's the truth."

Well, the knitters weren't going to make any issue of our short hair after Bud spoke up; they love Bud.

Bud, who is definitely what you'd call a rooster, has joined our knitting circle permanently. So with him here, it's not a real hen party anymore. He's here for practical reasons. Every year for the past four years, Bud has run for the Third District seat on the Lawrence County Board of Supervisors. The Third District seat kept getting vacated early because the old roosters holding office kept dying of old age midterm. Since Mr. Beckett didn't die midterm, like the rooster before him did, this is a regular election for a full-term seat. Ayma says that one of these years Bud is finally going to win.

He makes up these blue-and-white signs that say:

HALE YES!
Elect Bud Hale County Board
(paid for by Bud Hale)

Every year, the county votes *Hale No!* But he never gives up.

Of course, all we knit is campaign scarves for Bud in his trademark royal blue. When each scarf is done, Ayma or one of the ladies adds white stitching with the words *Hale Yes!*

Bud asked the ladies to knit the scarves for him, but then he ended up joining in the effort. Now, every Wednesday Bud shows up and knits and asks about Mom. He says he knits with us because he figures he needs a little church himself. None of us thought Bud would turn into a true knitter. We all figured it was Bud just trying to keep a line open to Mom and that is what really got him here the first time.

Since the ladies are ditching regular Wednesday night church to look after me, they place great emphasis on praying with every stitch they knit. In our knitting circle, all of our stitches are little prayers, and any kind of prayer will do. Whether you cast on a prayer for forgiveness or a prayer for thanksgiving makes no difference. You might be needing some help or even needing some specific thing, though I am careful not to be greedy by asking for things that I don't truly need, such as an iPod. An iPod is more of a want. I have a long list of prayers when I knit.

My knitting prayers include:

1. Let me belong in Wren.
2. Let Mom figure out how to belong in Wren, too.
3. Could Bud win a seat on the Board of Supervisors this time, please?
4. Please let beef prices stay up for a few more weeks until we can get to Cullman.
5. Keep Dixie protected when school starts.
6. Turn Delta into a sweet kid. Don't let him grow up like I think he is going to grow up—a seriously deranged person.
7. Bring Mom and Bud back together, maybe.
8. Thank you for sending Awanita to me.
9. I love my new muscles; help me keep getting stronger.
10. Please help me keep up with Bud in the field tomorrow.

The knitting and praying don't completely fix anybody. Still, I can see that being together with everyone helps all of us. There are six or seven of us who knit together, including Ayma, Bud, and me. Madilee Simms and Louisa Wilson are regulars, too. Most of the ladies are in their seventies or eighties. They have all known Mom since she was born, and they are not at all bashful about thinking that they know me, too, through osmosis, I guess.

The ladies have all known Bud for as long as they've known Mom. He is almost like one of the ladies himself. Because he is a big man in every way, Ayma has him knit with thick yarn and big needles—number seventeens. Otherwise, his hands would fumble around and he wouldn't make any progress.

Since Bud is using bigger needles than the rest of us, his scarves knit up a lot faster than everybody else's. Bud can knit up almost two complete scarves in a single night. The scarves are giveaways when he does his stump speeches. He thinks he is going to win this year. He thinks that every year, so I am told.

At knitting circle, you can count on hearing a lot of laughing and crying. Nobody minds sharing their stories of childbirth and menopause, and everything in between, even with Bud in the room. Bud doesn't tell his own stories of hardship and heartbreak, but you know he has them by the way he nods at the ladies when they talk, like he understands. Every now and again he'll say something meaningful like, "I know that feeling myself" or "Louisa, that story helps me—thank you."

Of course, every week the knitters want to know if

Bud has talked to Mom. I was surprised to hear that Bud and Mom have been e-mailing about the job opening in the Black Warrior. The ladies also take turns asking if there is any progress with Dixie and Delta. Like I said, there is no holding back in this crowd.

Someone usually asks Bud, "How is that sweet little girl of yours? Is she making any progress?"

Or another lady might need an update on Delta, but he doesn't get called sweet. "Bud, how're you doing with Delta? I know you've got your hands full with that one, yes, sir," is what Madilee said last time.

Bud answers the same way every time, as if he is hearing their questions for the first time and like he is genuinely happy they asked. "Oh, we're doing all right. I sure do appreciate your asking," he might answer.

Or he might really get them going by answering, "Every day things get a little easier, and for that I'm thankful."

The ladies love to hear Bud talk like that, about him being thankful. I am thankful too, thankful they have all stopped asking me if I wipe from front to back.

At knitting circle, the ladies tell how they have dealt with hardship and I can see that every one of them has overcome some real suffering in her life. I can also see that not one of the knitters has given up. That's why the knitting circle is good for me, even if it is a little bit like church.

CHAPTER TWENTY

SEEING HOW this is the last weekend before school starts, tonight I am staying the night with Dixie at Bud's. I haven't had a spend-the-night friend since Krystal and I were best friends in fourth grade. I am glad to have a true friend again. Bud says that the lady from the county who sees Dixie thinks it helps her to do normal girl things. Lots of normal girls have sleepovers.

While Bud fixes supper, he shoos Dixie, Delta, and me outside. Dinner is most likely going to be Bud's Brunswick stew, because that's about all Bud knows how to make.

"Go on out there to the barn and clean up them stalls," he orders the three of us.

Dixie whinnies and nods that she is happy to do that. Delta starts complaining about *Does he have to go with us? Can't he just watch TV?* Bud gives him eyes that I have hardly ever seen from Bud, but recognize from getting some similar eyes myself, from Mom. It works, too, because Delta hushes up and follows Dixie and me to the barn.

The Hales have four horses, so there is a good bit of work to be done before dinner. Ayma told me that they have four horses because there were four of them in the family, and they each had their own. Secret is Dixie's horse and is the exact equine image that I imagine Dixie to be. She's not quite fifteen hands, but is a sturdy, strong quarter horse. She's all chestnut with a black mane and a pure, white star in the middle of her forehead.

As comfortable and familiar as Sue and I are with each other, Dixie and Secret are even more so. I know that Sue trusts me, and I think I can feel that she has some mothering instincts about me. When I watch Secret and Dixie together, in the paddock or in the barn, I can see them talking with each other. Dixie only ever rides Secret bareback, totally bareback. I mean she uses no saddle, bridle, reins, or halter. Dixie barely holds Secret's mane, and they run together through all the fields. Anybody can see that they belong together.

Starlett's horse, Riddle, is the extra one now. Bud won't sell him because he says Riddle is not his to sell. But he won't ride him or care for him, either. Bud acts like Riddle is not here at all, Dixie is supposed to tend to him. Bud doesn't even look in his direction. Delta, on the other hand, gets downright ornery with Riddle.

In the barn before dinner, what actually happens is that I clean stalls while Dixie and Delta mess around being Dixie and Delta. Delta bounces around, being loud and obnoxious, getting in my way. Dixie, of course, curls up with Secret, who is lying down in her stall.

When Dixie lies down with Secret, Delta looks at the two of them with disgust. Then he looks to me as if I should be disgusted, too. Even though summer is technically over because school starts Monday, there are still flies everywhere, especially on the floor of Secret's stall, where they like to lay their eggs. Of course, the flies move out of Dixie's way when she curls up with Secret; they settle back down once Dixie settles. Secret flicks them off with her tail. Dixie doesn't mind or doesn't notice.

"She ain't always been this way," Delta says. "She was normal. She talked normal and acted normal when my mama was here."

I have a hard time imagining Dixie being a regular girl. Watching Dixie now with her horse, I understand that she's not pretending. This horse business is not a game to her.

"When was that, Delta? How old were you then?" I ask him.

"I was just a baby, but Bud told me."

I think it is entirely bratty when kids call their parents by their first names. My mom would have a cow if I called her Bye. Bud doesn't seem to care. Dixie doesn't call Bud anything. Sometimes she nuzzles him, though, and makes that rumbling sound that Secret makes when she and Dixie are curled up together.

I watch Secret and Dixie in the stall together and think how Dixie must be aching for her mother. My mom has only been gone for six weeks, and I have been longing for her something fierce since the very second she left. If I think for more than a minute or two about Mom being gone, my chest starts to hurt, so I try not to think about her much.

Secret is right here mothering Dixie, nuzzling her, and caring for her every day. No wonder Dixie is a horse. I say to Delta, "Secret acts like a mother to Dixie, doesn't she?"

Delta doesn't answer me. He stands at the door of Secret's stall, tossing poo at the two of them. I tell Delta to stop it and get him to help me turn the other three horses out so we can clean their stalls. Secret and Dixie are still spooned, so I skip over Secret's stall.

Once the other horses are out in the paddock, I hand Delta a shovel and make him go on and fill up a wheelbarrow with pine shavings from behind the barn. Bud likes to keep a thick blanket of pine on the floor of each stall because it absorbs the urine and also provides a good cushion for the horses' feet and makes for a cozier bed.

"You're not the boss of me, you know. I ain't doing it because you said to. If I do it, it's because Bud said to," Delta says when I tell him to help me.

"Okay, then," I say. "Get the shavings because Bud said to."

I don't care why Delta helps. I only care that he does so, because otherwise he will get carried away and keep teasing Dixie.

I give Delta the crappy job. I am halfway tempted to keep the shoveling for myself for the reasoning that shoveling totally builds upper-body strength and I'm keeping with my program of laser-like focus on being a strong girl. One thing I've learned from all of my muscle research is that every workout really just simulates the work that people used to do when they worked for real—on the land or building houses and railroads. A chore like shoveling, for example, engages all of the muscles in the arms, chest, shoulders, and back, so part of me doesn't want to give up this chore to Delta.

The rickety plastic wheelbarrow is what makes getting the shavings a sucky chore. The screw that held the wheel axle in place is long gone. Bud has the axle rigged with twine cut from a hay bale. The thing won't even roll forward when it's weighted down with shavings. To get it to move at all, you have to walk backward, kind of dragging it along and coaxing it not to fall over to the left. Handling the shavings would be way easier for me than it would be for Delta. But he needs some building up because he is one of those tiny boys. Struggling with a heavy, disabled wheelbarrow will do him good.

In the time it takes me to finish raking the manure from three stalls, Delta doesn't even get one load of shavings inside. We need six loads in all to make each stall perfect. "Delta? How ya coming with the shavings?" I holler when I go out to empty the manure.

"Hey!" he yells. "Get Dixie and come out here. I found something."

Dixie hears him, and we both go see what's up, because any time Delta finds something, you had better watch it.

Delta stands over a frightened chipmunk that he has

cornered and lodged between the barn, the wheelbarrow, and his shovel. "Cute, huh?" Delta says.

The chipmunk is cute — and scared enough that it can't move. I kneel down to see it better. Chipmunks are so good at hiding and disappearing that you usually can't get close to one, like you can with squirrels. My chest starts to hurt.

"Leave it alone. Let it go," I say.

I can't breathe; Delta laughs. I remember the first night I met Delta, when he tore up all those lightning bugs.

Delta raises his shovel and jams it into the chipmunk, cutting it in half.

Blood spatters the barn and my face. I look up for something; I can't breathe. There is exactly half a moon somewhere in the sky; I know because I watched it the whole walk over here tonight. The moon is nowhere to be seen in the sky right now. There's no air.

A deep roll starts from somewhere below my stomach — someplace I did not even know existed. I think oxygen would help me; I cannot breathe.

I puke onto half of the chipmunk. I try holding back the rest of it by thinking about the missing moon, but the rancid thoughts bubbling up from my stomach break against me until they spill out again through my mouth and my nose and it feels like even my eyes.

Dixie rears back and strikes Delta with her front hooves.

"Hey! What?" Delta cries.

What I want to do is cut Delta in half with a shovel. I picture the shovel again, and before I can make it stop, I picture myself cutting Delta in half. I lean against the barn, and straddling the chipmunk, which, at least, is now completely covered up, I vomit all over my boots. Dixie wipes my face with her shirt. I run to the gate toward the house without bringing in the horses or finishing the stalls. Dixie follows behind me. Delta runs after us, all the while yelling, "What? It's no big deal. Geez, it was a lousy chipmunk."

Bud stands at the gate, watching. Delta runs right past him. "Come on," Bud says, "time to eat."

Nobody speaks to Delta through all of dinner. One thing with Delta is that you don't have to tattle on him. He is so ignorant that first thing he does is tell on himself to Bud. He doesn't even think he did anything wrong. Dixie and Bud leave Delta in the kitchen to eat his dinner in solitary. They eat in the den. I can't eat, but go upstairs to shower.

I set the water extra hot in order to scorch the chipmunk off of my face. Then I scrub the washcloth extra hard over my eyes and forehead, until my skin can't take any more scrubbing. I keep my eyes open, so that I only see what is before me and not what happened in the barn. When I wash my hair, I don't shut my eyes. I don't mind the shampoo in them; it stings but it cleanses them good.

Now I try to think of Mom. I wonder if she is lonely or thinking of me. I imagine that I am in the field with Sue. I lean into her and breathe in her coat. I feel her ear twitch on my neck. I smell the dried earth that is in every part of Sue. I breathe with her so sweetly that I close my eyes; then the chipmunk pops in again. I stand under the force of the water until it turns ice cold.

Dixie and I are sleeping together in her room since there is no guest room at Bud's. She has a double bed, like I do. My stomach growls a little from missing supper. I think of Mom and Sue. Then I think of the shovel.

After a while, I hear Bud and Dixie go out to the barn to finish our chores. There is a lot left for them to do: get the shavings in the stalls, fill the water buckets, bring the horses inside for the night, and give them their grain. I try to talk myself into helping them, but I only want to think about Mom. Maybe my thoughts will reach her in Virginia. I send my spirit-self to be with her. My body-self tries hard to keep my eyes open. The shovel coming down will not leave my mind; when it does, I can't breathe. I turn on the ceiling fan and open the bedroom windows. I need air, and the half-moon is still hiding.

Sometime in the night, Dixie slips in through the doorway, which I left half open for her. She senses that I am awake and rumbles at me. I scoot over to make room for her in the double bed. She pushes my head with her nose to see if I am all right. I rumble back at her, and finally, I fall asleep with my friend Dixie wrapped around me.

CHAPTER TWENTY-ONE

FIRST THING THIS MORNING, Dixie and I are going to check on the baby deer together. By the time we get over to Ayma's, she has made us a breakfast of biscuits, honey, and blackberry tea. We're getting an early start because even now the heat is near ninety degrees and there is never a shortage of humidity in Alabama. While we eat, it's still dark outside and feels like the middle of the night to me.

Ayma sits down with us, and when she takes off her apron, chunks of biscuit dough fall on the floor. The house is dark, except for the kitchen. The three of us are quiet, too, except that Dixie makes an agitated rumbling noise when Ayma gets up to pull more hot biscuits from the oven. Ayma grins and kisses the top of Dixie's head.

Despite her being a horse, Dixie and I have become best friends. I've completely come to accept it; the girl is a horse. I don't mean she likes horses a lot — it's even more than being horse crazy. But, anyway, it's okay by me, because I like horses.

Even when they're behind a fence, horses seem free and wild, almost like they choose to stay put. You know they could jump over whatever pretends to hold them. I like how they reach out to people who are nice to them and how, if you pay attention, they tell you exactly what they think of you. All of that is just like Dixie.

We have figured out a way of talking that we both understand. Mostly, I use Dixie's horse gestures and sounds to get her attention or make an extra-enthusiastic point. I still do all of my serious talking in people-talk. She understands me and listens, but only ever replies in Horse. Ours is as easy a friendship as I've ever known. We can even argue in Horse, which involves a lot of foot stomping and blowing air out of our noses, with head tosses thrown in for emphasis.

Even though she doesn't talk at all, I believe that I am Dixie's one true friend, not counting her real horse, Secret. I believe that we are true friends because she told me so.

Dixie can speak regular if she wanted to; she just doesn't. I know because yesterday when I sat down next to her at Bud's, Dixie handed me a neatly folded note written on loose-leaf notebook paper:

> *You're my best friend. Thank you.*
> *Please come to my house again.*
>   *Dixie Hale*
> *P.S. A long time ago, my daddy almost*
> *married your mama. We are like sisters.*

Of course I immediately tried to ask her about Mom and Bud, but she just cantered away. I wonder if Dixie's right.

Anyway, I don't care one bit whether Dixie ever says one real out-loud word about Mom and Bud or anything else. I like hanging around her, and we have a lot of fun together, riding our bikes and picking on Delta. We *are* like sisters.

The sun is barely peeking out by the time we're done eating, and Ayma takes extra care getting us ready to go.

"Take care of Mary Harold if you go into the forest today," Ayma urges Dixie.

Dixie whinnies.

I protest, "I'll be okay. Nobody has to protect me."

Dixie canters off toward Sue's field and the forest so fast that as I follow her, I have to hold my hat on with one hand to keep it from flying off. I am bursting to see if Awanita is still nursing Sue. We stop at the back field, where we have the calves and their mothers separated from the bull. When we do finally see them, Awanita is pulling hard on Sue's teats. Sue doesn't seem to mind at all; she keeps on grazing. Looking at Awanita in the field, you wouldn't know that he lost his mother. He looks like he belongs here; he is a strong little buck. He walks with steady legs and nurses with furious intent. If Sue takes even a step or two away from him, Awanita bawls for her return. He sounds like a crazy meowing kitten.

Sometimes, I am learning, calves will steal milk from whichever cow they can. Usually, it takes at least a couple of tugs before the nursing cow figures out there is a little thief at her bag. Once she realizes it's not her child, a mama cow might kick the strange calf off and make a big fuss. Awanita eats as much as he wants, and Sue doesn't fuss at all.

Awanita looks up right at me. His face is all white, covered with Sue's milk, which is dripping off his chin like a spigot left running, as if he is Sue's blood calf. He nurses from her more than any other calf in the field is nursing right now, like he is missing something and is hoping to find it in Sue.

I was that way nursing, too. When I was a newborn, Mom says, I would nurse for hours at a time, until she was completely drained and would have to ask Ayma to hold me to her breast. Ayma would crawl into the bed facing Mom and prop me up while I nursed so that Mom could go back to sleep. For the whole first three months of my life, Ayma and Mom nursed me like that because, like Awanita, I was so hungry.

I could stand here watching Sue and her baby for the entire morning. Dixie is getting restless; she wants to swim in the Sipsey River. Awanita follows me through the field; I tell him not to worry about me—I'll be back soon.

CHAPTER TWENTY-TWO

THIS BEING THE NEXT-TO-LAST DAY before school, Dixie and I are spending the whole day together at the Sipsey River without Delta. Like usual, Delta begs to tag along with us; we don't let him. We forbid Delta to come with us because he is a violator. He breaks the rules of the forest. He drops trash, pulls up entire plants, and moves too many rocks; he kills things.

I would never kill a spider for spinning a web in a horse stall. I wouldn't smush a frog or a mouse for the sport of it, either. I must confess that I do kill mosquitoes. I slap them hard after they bite me—I can't seem to help it. But Delta is trouble, and after what he did to that poor chipmunk, there's no way we're bringing him with us to the Sipsey River.

Swimming at the Sipsey River picnic areas is sort of a compromise between Dixie and me. Dixie would prefer to be running around in the forest trying to find new waterfalls. I would rather be home with Sue and Awanita.

To me, the forest is tick heaven these days. Also it scares me because you can't really see a lot of sky when you're in it. Plus I can't breathe right in the forest because I get afraid that I might get lost. Not to mention that in this heat and humidity there is no good air for me when I do start feeling tight in the chest. If I'm too far into the forest, I worry I won't find my way out in time to breathe.

Dixie's more like Mom; she loves that forest and knows her way around just like she was an old lady driving to the courthouse for the gazillionth time. I'm sure Dixie could find us a much better swimming hole than the Sipsey picnic area, but it would be too far in for me. We agree to swim here near the parking lot until I get a little more acclimated.

What I like about this part of the Sipsey is that it's deep enough to float in but shallow enough to see the bottom. Dixie loves to float on her back. She's not like a horse when she's in the river. She floats with her eyes closed, without even the littlest bit of worry on her face.

I wonder what Dixie's thinking about when she floats and I wonder what will ever make her talk. The only thing that could have made me talk again, in Virginia, would have been feeling safe and maybe like I was part of something. How could I have ever felt safe there again? I wonder if Wren feels unsafe for Dixie. I hope not.

Even if we get to be old ladies and she's still neighing and whinnying, that'll be all right with me. I will love Dixie forever for understanding that the forest scares me sometimes. I will love her for reminding me how to be friends.

While Dixie floats near the right bank, I watch a snake pop up on the other side of the river. I breathe and watch. I helped Mom with a wildlife display last year. I could be staring at a cottonmouth. Mom would know for sure and I'm not expert, but I'm relying on those round eyes and wormy head to keep me from worrying too much. I wade over between Dixie and the snake. The snake is far enough away that I feel like this is a good time for me to practice my new trait of being brave.

I check out my muscles; I think they are getting bigger. Using Ayma's turtle-slow Internet connection to help me research the fastest way to get strong, I have made myself a crazy workout routine to build up my muscles. The whole thing is built on push-ups and pull-ups, and it's obvious that my push-ups and pull-ups have made a serious difference in my strength. I intend to keep building up, though I'm already looking pretty buff. There's a picture of my perfect muscles in this week's *Lawrence County Bulletin*. They've got a whole story about Bud and me trying to save Sue's calf, then losing it, and me finding Awanita. I'm going to send a copy to Mom. She'll be surprised at how different I look and not just because of my pixie haircut.

The headline of this article is OH, DEER! Bud thinks that is the funniest thing he has ever read. I think it's stupid. Bud is going around saying, "Oh, deer!" every time he sees me.

The caption below the picture reads:

Bud Hale (Woods Farm Manager and 3rd District Board of Supervisors independent candidate) of Wren, and Miss Mary Harold Woods (daughter of Tabythia Nelson Woods, granddaughter of the late Harold Burrell Woods and Mrs. Mary Nelson Woods), also of Wren, with Sue and her adopted calf, Awanita.

Bud looks likes a complete goofball in the picture, wearing his baseball cap and one of the Hale Yes! campaign scarves, when it's the middle of August. I look good in the picture because my short hair is awesome-looking. All the other girls around here wear their hair longish. In the picture, I'm wearing short sleeves and my biceps and shoulders are totally ripped; I can even see the outline of my deltoids.

I am up to about a hundred push-ups every day. I do fifty in the morning and fifty at night. The bar in my closet makes an excellent pull-up bar, too. If I start from a halfway position, I can do twenty. If I start out from a fully extended position and try to get my chin above the bar, I can do nine true pull-ups. At the beginning of the summer, I could do exactly zero. I also about passed out after holding only one fence post back then, too.

Thinking about how strong I am makes me not scared of this snake at all. I imagine myself calm and strong facing the snake; all of this imagining has a pretty good effect. I watch the snake glide away upstream. I look over at Dixie; she is still floating with her eyes closed. Part of me wants her to know that I just saved us from a snake; part of me wants to let Dixie have her peace in the river. I wonder if she thinks in English or Horse.

"Last one in is a shit sandwich!" I hear hooting and hollering in the parking lot, making its way toward us. A bunch of boys have shown up. One of them yells above the others.

Dixie's eyes shoot open and she is up, out of the water, out of her world, and standing behind me. I size them up as they push and shove each other all the way down the bank. Two of them look about Dixie's age; the other two are my age, or a little older. The loud boys see her.

"Hey there, horse girl," the oldest one, with the gravelly voice, taunts. "Come on and swim with us. You know we won't hurt you."

My strength and my courage glide away, upstream with that wormy-looking snake. I want to run from them and take Dixie, too. She is crouching low behind me, trying to hide. Dixie blows on my leg. I am her alpha horse, and she is asking for my protection.

I don't know what they have done to her before now. I never ever want to know, but I see they have hurt her.

These boys are different from that snake, and I'm of a mind to disappear now. I almost run; I almost leave Dixie to fend for herself. Then I remember why I came to Wren. I think about how strong and beautiful I felt the day I freed my hair, and myself, from, Krystal and Virginia. I push down Krystal and her black ribbons, the chocolate-milk cartons, and everything else. That's all six hundred ninety-one miles away. I push it way down inside. I pack away all of Virginia, except for Mom, tightly away so that it can never get out again.

I hold my seashell necklace because it's the next closest thing to Mom; she told me to watch over Dixie. Mom said I get to be somebody new, whoever I want to be. The day I cut my hair, I decided to speak up for myself. Right now, I decide that includes Dixie, too.

Then my nose stops inhaling.

Ayma says God gives us everything we need to get through. I can't freaking breathe. Bud says letting go is not the same as giving up.

My chest threatens to cave in, and I can feel my fear of dying starting to rise. I look up. I look up so I won't fall into the earth. There are trees, with so many green leaves I don't bother to even try to identify them, but there is more sky than leaves. There is plenty of blue, open sky with that slice of waxing moon like I saw that day with Mom at Rattlesnake Creek. Oh, I love a daylight moon.

I want to live in Wren; I am choosing something new. My damn nose won't inhale. I open my mouth.

I open my mouth to breathe, and I speak. Without a stutter or a quake, I speak.

"Y'all go on home, if you're going to act like assholes," I say clearly. Dixie runs up to stand on the left bank, leaving me thigh-deep in the river with these four boys. No one can believe that I just called them assholes; I sure can't.

147

One of them whistles at me.

"What?" says the big one. "I didn't hear you."

I open my mouth again. This time I breathe in before I speak. Then I say, "Leave." I breathe out. These boys are bullies, and my time of tolerating bullies has ended.

The boy laughs with a big, head-tossing laugh. He gets all tough and says, "Make me leave, Butch."

I'm learning that new muscles are funny. They like being used at every opportunity. When the boy says, "Make me," and calls me that name, my biceps start itching and my pecs do, too. My Ayma spot itches; I ignore it. Scratching right now will make me look like a wuss.

I've never tangled with a person. The other day I did wrestle a three-hundred-pound steer into the chute, though. I thought that calf was going to kick my ass. Then Bud started telling me how we had eighty head left to work, and if I was going to spend all morning on this one calf, he might as well drive the thirty minutes to Decatur to that new Starbucks for a latte, then come on back and check on me. He said he might even get himself a scone, too, because he'd been wanting to try one. Then he muttered to nobody, "What the hell is a scone, anyway?"

Bud would no more step foot in a Starbucks than Mom would eat at a Hooters. He was just trying to fire me up. Bud doesn't understand the depth of my ability to tolerate idiots. I've had a lot of practice. Plus Bud and I are on the same team, so he wasn't rattling me as much as he thought he was.

Bud was leaning on the fence, grinning like crazy in the shade, not sweating a trickle, and he would not let up until I sent that calf down to him. Not only did I wrestle the calf to the ground; I finally put him in a headlock, slammed him into the chute door, twisted his tail, and made him trot all the way to Bud at the head gate like we were bound together in a three-legged race. Was I bruised, sprained, pulled, and swollen the next morning? To borrow a phrase from Bud, *Hale yes*.

Standing here in the Sipsey River, I size up this loudmouthed boy picking a fight with me now. He weighs a good deal more than I do, but not nearly as much as the calf I corralled. I could take him, but I won't start the fight.

The boy smirks at me. "That's what I thought." He dismisses me with a toss of his head toward his buddies. They turn to Dixie, who's been watching us from the riverbank.

I step between them.

"Move!" the boy orders me.

"Make me," I say. My nose is with the program now. I am breathing on my own, and my brain is occupied with getting Dixie and myself out of this mess.

If I have learned one thing so far, it's that finding a good, true friend is rare and wonderful. A true friend will stick by you when you're in trouble. She'll overlook your faults and give you a second chance after a misunderstanding. And most important, an honest-to-goodness friend will step up and help you get yourself right. Dixie and I are good and true friends; I protect her and she protects me. It wasn't long ago that I couldn't even protect myself. I will stand here today, and I will protect both of us.

The boy pushes me, and I am ready. I have taken more force mending fences. I hardly move when he makes contact with my shoulders.

My turn.

I imagine that he is a steer. I imagine moving him into the last part of the chute. He falls into the river on contact. I surprise myself, not with my strength but with the low growl that comes out of me when I shove him. I sound like Hoss, our bull.

His friends start laughing, and the boy calls me all the names I have heard about myself since the fourth grade. I don't hit him again, though I imagine that, too, and it would feel good to bust his face and teach him a lesson. I hold myself back from giving him a good lesson. I talk myself down from striking him over and over, and as soon as I don't, I regret it because I figure that if I did really pound him, he might actually leave Dixie and me alone forever.

The gravelly-voiced boy starts talking about kicking my ass, but his friends won't let him fight a girl. Dixie stands on the bank until she is sure they are gone for good, then she joins me again in the river.

I float on my back like Dixie does, then turn into the dead man's float for a long time. I flip back over and keep my eyes open and try to get lost in the sky. The forest canopy is not scary from here; there are lots of tiny blue birds up there in the treetops. I hear them singing to us: *Zi ZHEE ZHEE ZIZIZIZI zzzzeeet.* I don't know what kind of birds they are. Mom would know; so would Ayma.

Dixie floats beside me. We hold hands so that we don't float away from each other. I'm not going to let go of Dixie; I'm going to stick with her.

When we get home, there is our baby deer, standing right where we left him, waiting for our return. When he sees me, he starts ramming his head into Sue's side and Sue walks away. He meows for her until she gives in and comes back to her rambunctious baby, letting him nurse again, as much as he wants.

Chapter Twenty-three

TODAY WE'RE FINISHING UP on giving the cows all their shots since we plan on taking them to auction at Cullman next week. School starts tomorrow, and even though Ayma is not crazy about me working on a Sunday, she agreed to let me be out here with Bud because once I'm in school, I'll have less time to help out.

Our farm is just the starter farm for the cows. We try to grow the very best cows possible, then we sell them at Cullman. The next cattleman, somewhere in the middle of the country or out West, grows them even bigger, then sells them for beef. Even though this is my very first season, I know what it means to take them to Cullman. I try not to think about it, and at the same time, every time I send one of these cows through the chute, I am telling each one of them *thank you.*

Bud and I don't talk about this, because I know what he will say. He'll talk to me about acceptance. He'll talk to me about gratitude and honoring life. Bud will listen to everything I have to say and then he will get quiet and ask me what do I think? So instead of asking him, I just decide to love each and every one of these cows — the ones with names and the ones with numbers — until it's time for them to go to Cullman. Only I will never send Sue to Cullman.

I saw Number Forty-eight this morning without a calf beside her; we've been expecting her to drop a calf anytime. Her bag was so grotesquely engorged that it was downright shocking to me that she had no calf tugging at her. She shouldn't be full of milk if there's not a calf yet. I spent a long time walking the fields looking for her dead baby or a sick live one, but nothing was out there, anywhere. We're watching that mama cow because something's not right with her or her bag. Number Forty-eight needs to get healthy soon so she can stay here with us; it's too early to be thinking about sending her to Cullman. She's only three years old; Number Forty-eight ought to live on Wren Mountain ten or twelve more years.

None of our cows get the hormone shots, like those at Beckett's Cow Palace in Moulton Valley do. Ayma doesn't believe in giving cows hormone shots to make them bigger; neither does Bud. Ours only get vaccines to keep them healthy and antibiotics to cure them if they're sick. The big pain about giving the shots is that you have to get the entire herd into a pen, then send them down the chute and one at a time fix them into the headlock. Today we're doing our cows and Bud's at the same time; that's a hundred fifty-three head to be worked.

Bud likes to vaccinate the calves first because the rest of the herd knows what is coming and they've learned, over the years, to cooperate. The calves pitch a big, fat fit, and so we try to get them out of the way. Getting the calves in from the field is easier if they're with the baby-sitters. The babysitters are the heifers, girls who have never calved. They take the babies down to the creek or to the shady part of the field to take care of them. I guess this is how the heifers get their practice for when they will become cows. Sue doesn't let the babysitters take Awanita from her.

Sue is such a trusting old girl that we give her shots to her right in the field. She doesn't run or swing her head like she's getting ready to charge the way some of the other cows do. Sue and Awanita get special treatment; we don't separate them from each other. Of course, we don't vaccinate Awanita; he doesn't get an ear tag, either.

Today Awanita keeps his distance from me. He bleats so loudly when I move near him that Bud teases me and I get embarrassed. "He's fussing at you, Cricket! What'd you do wrong?"

Then it does almost sound like Awanita's telling on me; he doesn't make that sweet meowing sound anymore; it's almost like he's calling for Ayma! *AAAyuuuh, AAAyuuuh, AAAyuuuh,* the deer cries at such a high pitch that all the babysitters start coming unnerved.

I'm pretty sure Dixie wouldn't have told on me about shoving that mean boy at the Sipsey yesterday, and even if she would have told, Bud doesn't understand Horse the way I do. I did see the intolerable Delta slinking around where we were swimming, so I know he followed us.

I just stop looking at Awanita altogether and change the subject off of me and onto Bud. While I'm trying to get a pinkeye vaccine into the muscle of a heifer, I ask Bud, "Why do you keep running for office if you're just going to lose?"

Before he answers, Bud gives me a good hard look in the face. "Because I'm a patriot, champ." To Bud, everybody is a champ.

"Patrick Henry was a patriot, Bud. You're a country

boy working cows on Wren Mountain." I like getting Bud all fired up, and it's easy to do.

Bud gets riled about that; now he wants to talk politics. Most often when we're working cows, Bud and I don't converse. You can't let yourself get complacent; you can't ever forget that these are thousand-pound animals. There's not much time for real talking because you have to pay close attention in the field and in the chute.

Today, though, he jumps down off the fence, leaving one of the girls locked in the head gate, mooing like crazy. He gets right up in my face, not in a threatening way, but in kind of a lunatic way, with spit flying and arms flapping everywhere. "That's right! That's right, that's right!" he hollers.

When Bud gets excited, he kind of repeats himself until his mouth catches up with his brain. He is talking so fast, I fear he might fall down on account of getting himself off balance. Bud made the chute himself, and it is not the prettiest or the strongest one ever made. He talks big about reinforcing it or making some kind of improvements with rebars and wood planks, but at this moment things are pretty wobbly out here.

"Cricket, I am a country boy. That's exactly why I run, and why I will run until I win. Hale, yes! Because like Patrick Henry and Ben Franklin, and your boy

T.J."—he thinks Thomas Jefferson is my boy because I lived in Virginia—"I am a country boy who loves this little mountain and wants to make it better. I—"

"Okaaay. I get it." I stop Bud before he really does make himself fall over.

Besides, I've studied American history more recently than Bud probably has. I refrain from reminding him that T.J. was not a country boy but a country gentleman who liked to decorate houses and kept hundreds of slaves to work his own little mountain.

Bud keeps on rolling: "Things need changing around here. Some people don't think about Wren and what Wren needs. Some people only think about themselves; they make laws that bring them money but harm the land. That ain't right."

I guess he's talking about Mr. Beckett, the same Mr. Beckett of the cow palace, and how the board passed a law that allows farmers to use sludge on their fields, or maybe how Mr. Beckett voted to pave over parts of the Old Town Path, an old Indian trail. I have heard all about Mr. Beckett.

"You watch—I'll win one of these days!" Bud holds up the syringe and squirts out the vaccine to give an exclamation point to his speech, then in two leaps he is on the fence. He talks about his platform for another hour, at least, all the while comparing himself to Thomas Jefferson.

After struggling to get some of the young steers down the chute, Bud takes his cap off, wipes his forehead, and from out of nowhere, except maybe his mind has been burning on it, he says, "I know I'm an underdog in this race. I'm gon' win this year; I can feel it." Then he gets back to work.

Around Wren, Bud is a bit of an underdog, partly because he always loses the election, partly because Starlett ran off to Nashville, leaving him to raise Dixie and Delta on his own, and I guess partly because Dixie and Delta have their strain of peculiar.

We vaccinate all the cows before lunchtime, including Hoss, the bull. The bull is easy to get into the chute today because he is limping. That makes him weaker and not as quick to get away from us, though he's definitely more aggressive because he is in pain.

Today Hoss gets a third and final round of antibiotics. If he gets better, he'll stay on Wren Mountain with us. If not, it's off to Cullman. We can't keep a bull who can't do his job. Right now, Bud is not the only one in the underdog position.

I give extra thanks for Hoss, and while he is in the head gate, I talk to him. I don't talk to him out loud but in a heart way. I feel stupid, but I do it. I tell Hoss that everything will be okay no matter what happens. I don't know if I'm lying or not. I don't want to be lying; I urge Hoss to accept the antibiotics and get better. I tell him Wren Mountain is his home and he needs to get stronger if he is going to survive here.

Awanita and Sue stand far away from Hoss; the more aggressive the bull acts, the farther my deer retreats. When I call her over to me, Sue comes right up. I hold on to her. I am pretty sure that when Mom said owning a cow would be good for me, she didn't figure on Sue teaching me about breathing in and out.

Awanita cannot decide where he wants to be—with me or nearer the forest. I am aching to hold him close to me just one more time like I did when I found him. Finally, he shoves his head in my hand; I keep my eyes shut and breathe. I close my eyes and try to feel my new strong self in this body. There's no one here to call me home or to call me names. I stand in the field searching for what it is to be wild and calm and gentle and strong.

Chapter Twenty-four

THANKFULLY, DELTA IS NOT at my school. It's bad enough that he rides the same bus as Dixie and me, since our schools are right next door. That horrendous boy acts like a demon toward his own sister every day, which is one of the many reasons why somebody needs to bust Delta into his own sense. All I have to say is that Delta had better act right or he's in serious trouble with me.

Some people might say Dixie brings on the teasing and torment she gets by her refusal to just act like a girl. Those are the same people who would probably think that about me, too — that I caused all of my own problems in

Virginia. I say, no matter how strange Dixie, or anybody, acts, that's not a good reason for cruelty and torture. I'm glad I've grown strong, strong enough to protect myself and Dixie. Delta doesn't need protecting; what he needs is a good busting.

I'll get to put myself, and all my strength, to the test later this school year. A girl my age only has to do two pull-ups or the flexed arm-hang for about twenty seconds in order to pass the fitness test; doing the number I can do will be the best part of school, I think. Coach Simms, our PE teacher, who also happens to be the nephew of my knitting friend Madilee, the rolled-down stockings lady, is big on giving a physical fitness test to everybody.

It turns out that big old gravelly-voiced boy, the one I shoved at the river, is named Gil Traylor. He holds the school record for pull-ups; he did fifteen last year. I can already do thirteen. I want to beat Gil's record. Every day I plan on practicing my pull-ups during free period. That way, Gil can see me focused like a missile on his record.

Since fifth, sixth, and seventh grades have free period together, I can watch over Dixie while I train for the pull-up contest. For the most part, everybody else does their own thing out here. The popular girls stand around talking and sharing lip gloss, a disgusting habit which surely spreads germs and disease. The medium-popular girls walk around and around the yard, trying to look like popular girls, rubbing on even more lip gloss. Some boys are playing murder ball, which is exactly where I'd like to be but for the fact that I am in training.

Dixie minds her own business, cantering and trotting through the open pasture, which is nothing but a soccer field. She is free, roaming her own world with the wind in her face, the sunshine on her withers, and her long, muscled legs carrying her to a field far away. I always keep my eye on Dixie. I like to be sure that no one fouls her up. Mostly girls ignore Dixie, but some boys like to make sport of her because she is a horse.

I finish my sixteenth and record-breaking pull-up. Now I know I can win. It won't be official, though, unless I can get the job done on test day, too. I stop to catch my breath, stretching my lats, and look around for Dixie. Stretching is the best part of doing all this work. My back and shoulders release easily while I dangle from the bar. One by one, I feel each muscle in my back relax. I look through my arms, while I hang, trying to find Dixie.

On first glance, everything seems in order: girls talking, girls walking, murder ball.

Where is Dixie?

Hanging from the bar, I scan everyone again, until I finally spot her cornered against the school building, surrounded by Russell and Gil and a couple of stupid fifth-graders.

At our school the younger boys, mostly fourth-graders, race through the halls with their motors on, like they are some hotshot race-car drivers. Whenever one of those drivers cuts Dixie off, she rears up and neighs at him. If she has to wait too long in the cafeteria line, Dixie stomps her feet and blows air through her lips. If I pass her a note in the hall, she tosses her head back and whinnies at me. I don't ever whinny back at school, though I do toss my head now and again. She likes it when I do that.

Dixie even smells like a horse. You kind of get used to that smell, even start to crave it after a while. Plenty of folks in Wren have a horse or a mule or some kind of horse-like animal that they are attached to, for sure. Lots are in the 4-H and Future Farmers of America; practically everybody shows their livestock at some kind of fair or competition. You would think it's no big deal if one girl got carried away with herself. But it is a big deal.

The tormenting makes no difference to Dixie, because she knows that she is not the alpha horse. Dixie is part of the fifth-grade herd, and she is way, way down the line of dominants—at the bottom. I'm in the seventh grade, closer to the top. In our school herd, the teachers are the alphas most of the time because they protect Dixie from Russell and Gil, who are in my grade and only think they are the alphas.

Good alphas meet the needs of the entire herd; good alphas only bully others around when it's necessary for the common good. Russell and Gil care only for themselves and bully people for kicks, not for productivity's sake. They enjoy knocking Dixie's books out of her hands or pushing her to the ground when she's tying her shoes. Whenever they do these things, Dixie neighs, rears, and then canters off to the farthest point away from them. But today she's been trapped.

I feel like I've been here before, only back then I was in Dixie's place. Gil Traylor has got Dixie up against the wall of the school and is rubbing up on her with his hips. Two fifth-grade boys, trying to be all cool, but who are really just like those over-glossed girls, are cheering, "Horse girl, horse girl!" That seems such a stupid thing to chant; fifth-grade boys will do anything. Russell is egging them to keep it up. Then Dixie spits in Gil's face.

I hightail it over, but my ass-kicking face doesn't even scare those boys a bit. To protect herself, Dixie drops flat on her back with all four hooves in the air—the front two protecting her face and the bottom two kicking out whenever she can. She looks more like a crab than a horse.

True to herself and her genus, Dixie is fighting to the death, neighing angrily with all that her vocal chords can offer up. Still, they go at her with kicks and laughs and their ridiculous horse-girl chant. There is not a teacher in sight, so I do what needs to be done. Bud says that's called taking a leadership role, doing what needs to be done in tough situations.

I shock myself by neighing at them, like I am a horse, too. I'm sticking with Dixie. When they hear me, the stupid boys turn away from Dixie and start laughing at me instead. Dixie lifts her head, snorts at me, and rests her head back down with her two front hooves blocking her face again. My presence is only a minor distraction; the boys turn to Dixie again. This time, I stomp and rear and make louder, angrier horse sounds — mixed in with English so they are perfectly clear about my objective with them. "Back off her, or I'll kick your asses all to hell!"

This cracks them up, and while they are laughing, I do kick their asses like I said I would. Between me and those four boys, we stir up about a hundred times more dust and a million times more attention. Dixie has the horse sense to gallop off to the far end of the soccer field, isolating herself from us.

When I come home from school with a busted nose and a suspension note, Ayma seems more worried about my nose than about me being kicked out of school for a few days before the first week of school has even ended. Ayma tears up about it and says, "That's my Mary Harold, always for the underdog. You're a good girl."

I get that underdog business from Ayma; she insists on rooting for the ones with no one on their side. My nose hurts something fierce; I'll have a black eye tomorrow, for sure.

Before going to bed, I think about e-mailing Mom but change my mind. I'll tell Mom about my busted nose and all this trouble later. I even forgot to visit Sue and Awanita when I came home today. That's a lie. How could I forget? Bud moved all the cows and calves up here into the field beside the house; they are noisy, and Awanita is noisiest. He kept hollering, louder than ever, for Sue, even after the moon came up. Or maybe he was hollering after me.

Chapter Twenty-five

EVEN THOUGH SCHOOL HAS STARTED, on Saturday Dixie and I still ride our bikes to the Sipsey River. My nose is busted, and half of my face is all swollen from my playground domination of the other day, but Russell and Gil got it the worst. I only have one black eye, my left one.

Ayma has fixed Dixie and me picnic lunches and we'll spend the entire day in the forest, or at least on the edge of the forest. We'll have another month of Saturdays left to keep coming here. The river feels like bathwater to me, and being out here with Dixie is exactly what I need to relax from everything that happened at school.

Today, Dixie convinces me to go farther upstream than our usual swim spot. The 202 Trail, which runs beside the Sipsey, is well traveled for a couple of good miles, with plenty of waterfalls and ravines for Dixie that are still close enough to civilization and road access for me.

Still, Dixie would rather go off to some canyon that's so far off of any marked trail that it has no name, no number, and appears on no map.

Even though I know the road and two parking lots are only about fifty steps up the bank, I can't see all of that from here. The water runs warm and clear and reminds me of Rattlesnake Creek, only with more rocks and about twice as wide. The sun has done a nice job of heating up the Sipsey to where it feels like I am almost floating in air. On my back, I can only see a perfect circle of blue sky surrounded by the faces of hundreds of old trees looking down at me. The Sipsey makes me quiet inside.

In the river, Dixie and I are silent. We are together, each floating in our own imagination.

Even on the trail closest to the parking lot, you can see traces of the Sipsey all through the forest, over the rocks and ridges. Here, it showers down over top of a massive boulder; and for now it's content to do so, but there are cracks in the big boulder. Very slowly, the Sipsey River is making a canyon—the Great Sipsey Canyon—just a little ways from the parking lot. The future is easy to read: the boulder will come down. Day by day the river is cutting its path.

One day, one of my very own great-great-grandchildren—a girl, I'll bet—will be right here where I am. I bet some of my grandmothers stood here, too.

Maybe my great-great-granddaughter will have an ugly, crooked toe or a beauty mark on her leg. She will look up at the sky and just like me, she'll think how she loves to see a half-moon in the broad daylight. Just like me she will say to herself, I'm glad I don't live on a planet with sixteen moons, because that's just too many for one girl to befriend. One good old moon is the best, because you can really get to know it over your life. Then she'll look up at her moon, scratch her beauty mark, and whether she knows it or not, I'll be helping her find her way, same way Ayma helps me find mine.

It feels like way after noon by the time Dixie and I get hungry enough to eat. The Sipsey is no longer ours alone, but at least we got here early enough to put our stuff on the best spot. We share a blanket on the boulder that reaches out over the river. Not but a few bites into our tomato sandwiches, possibly the last good ones of this year, Dixie's eyes get so big that all you see is the white. Her nostrils flare up, too.

I get a sick wave in my stomach when I hear the emphysema voice of Gil Traylor. He is only fourteen, but it sounds like he has been smoking for forty years. Gil flunked the third grade, which means that even though he is in my same grade, he is a year older than I am. He lies about his age and says he started kindergarten late. Because he is such a bully, and everybody is afraid of him, nobody calls him on lying about flunking.

I've proven that I can take Russell and Gil both, but I don't feel like fighting today. I react too slowly; Dixie does, too. I guess, each in our own way, we get rattled by the sound, and thought, of meeting up with Gil and Russell out here alone.

"Hey, look, it's horse girl and the dyke from Virginia," says Russell. It's either my amazing spiky haircut or the fact that I kicked their asses that bothers them so much. I decide to take a breath and not get all fired up. Not just yet.

Dixie freezes. She stands behind me, waiting for safety. I ponder the situation. A part of me has a big itch to go on and get this over with, but the thing is, Dixie would probably get hurt, too. My nose and face are still hurting from the other day at school. The swelling has gone down some, but the top of my cheek still interrupts my line of vision. Even if I set my mind to carefully tangling with Russell and Gil, there'd be some pain involved for me, too. They'd probably go right for my face. That's what I would do to them if I were to take them on right now. Definitely, that's what I'd do, direct all my shots at their already banged-up faces.

"Hi, guys," I say, trying to chill them and myself out. "Great day for a swim."

What an idiotic thing to say. But I'm trying to find a way out. They are both perched on their bikes. Another option, of course, would be to kick one of them into the other. Though I have been working on developing my lower body by lunge-walking in the heifer field, I am not one-hundred percent certain that I have the leg strength to fully entangle them with one good kick, which is all I would get. We'd just be in a foot race, and lung capacity is my weak link in the fitness chain. But Dixie can out-run anybody.

Gil mocks me. "Great day for a swim," he says with serious exaggeration. "Aw, how did you hurt your nose? Get into a fight?"

"You know what?" I say. "We're not looking for another fight. We're just enjoying the river. Maybe you could leave us alone today," I tell both of them, but not in a begging way, more in a sort of businesslike, matter-of-fact way.

Russell cracks up and says to Gil, "Isn't that sweet? They want to be alone." He sorta whispers to Dixie, like it's a secret, "Your little brother told me about you two. I heard how you like to be alone." He makes air quotes around "alone."

"Yeah," Gil pipes up, "the little retarded kid told us all about you two."

When I get ahold of him later, Delta will be a sorry-ass boy for sure, but that's between Delta and me. My face is burning up now, not with pain so much anymore, but with anger that they think they can fling around any words they want about anybody, especially Delta. He is a demon boy, but he lives on Wren Mountain, so I'm sticking with him.

I take a step closer to Gil. "Shut up! Shut your pie-hole, and if you ever say that again, it will be the last time you say it."

Then Gil rolls his bike toward me, like we're swapping baseball cards or something. "How about we give you another black eye, just to even things up? Then we'll leave you two alone."

This is a total double shot of suck; anything I do is going to make my life worse and Dixie's, too. I could go ape shit on them. If I just lose it completely, like a nutcase, maybe they'll freak and just leave.

But I'm not a nutcase.

They are the ones who started all of this by being jackasses who think they can do whatever they want to any girl they want. Well, I won't let them do whatever they want to Dixie or me. I try to make a plan before I get myself into more trouble. The day I got suspended, I was awfully proud of cleaning up on those boys after what they had done to Dixie. Today I am tired, my face still hurts, and I realize already that this is not going to end here, no matter who gets an ass-kicking at the river.

Gil gets off of his bike and throws it to the ground. I think this is some kind of chest-pounding gorilla move designed to scare us. Russell throws his bike to the ground, too, and it's like the dance of the cauliflower head when he does. Everything about him is like that yellow-white vegetable, and his skin is that same kind of lumpy, too.

When Cauliflower Boy throws his bike down, I do the wrong thing for someone who is avoiding a fight. I fall out laughing. On the one hand, it's cool because Dixie laughs, too. Never in my life have I heard a horse laugh; only people laugh. Dixie's laughter makes me laugh even harder. I am laughing hard enough that tears are pouring down my face. I can see Russell Cauliflower winding up to sock me, but I cannot stop laughing 'cause, honest to goodness, his ears even flap a tad bit when he draws his arm back. I wait for the impact and try to plan what I'll do when it hits.

I find an opening in my breath enough to say one word to Dixie: "Run."

Dixie's the one who throws a kick hard into Gil's bike, and then she runs. Gil hits the ground, holding both his shins, and I try to think of my options quickly. I am too close to Russell to get in any good punches. I drop to the ground and wrap both of my legs tight around him and then he can't help but fall down. This is a fight that I won't win. I hold my own, sort of, meaning that I am able to protect my already busted face. But today the two of them are too much for me. Russell socks me hard in my chest and I keep on breathing.

Over my swollen cheeks, I see a familiar-looking uniform standing on the bank above us. Someone has called a forest ranger on us. Again I can only find one word: "Help."

Gil sees the ranger about the same time I do. He doesn't want to stick around. "Shit! Let's get out of here!" he hollers. The ranger doesn't even try to go after them, which kind of annoys me.

Because our farms are in the forest, the ranger knows Ayma and Bud. He loads my bike, and Dixie's, into his truck and carries me up the road. I convince him to drop me off at our driveway, and I promise that I will tell Ayma what happened.

Chapter Twenty-six

BY THE TIME I GET BACK HOME with our bikes, it is close to dark. Ayma is knitting on the screen porch. She calls out to me, "Where'd your horse friend run off to? I saw her galloping through the heifer field a bit ago."

"She got tired and came back early," I lie because I don't want to talk with Ayma about me fighting again. I kiss Ayma's cheek and brush past her before I get any more questions.

"Oh," Ayma says, surprised. "Why'd the ranger bring you home?"

The door slams behind me; I pretend not to hear. I'm sure she will have thought of plenty more questions by the time I get back.

Before changing out of my wet clothes, I e-mail
Mom:

Mom, I hate Ayma's dial-up. Rode bikes in the forest
and swam in the Sipsey. I like trails with blazes best.
Dixie is good at getting around. I pulled eight ticks off
me just now. I miss you. Love, Cricket

In my room at the dressing table, I look at myself in
the mirror to be sure that this fighting girl is me. I am
still shaking from our run-in with the boys. I probably
ought to do some pull-ups on the closet bar to get myself
right. I should at least do some push-ups, so I don't back-
slide from the training progress I've made. I totally want
to beat Gil's stupid pull-up record now. I am not having
trouble breathing; if anything, I am breathing too fast.

I don't do pull-ups or push-ups. Instead, I sit in front
of the mirror for a minute more. I don't look like me; I
don't know who I look like. I sort of don't even look like
a girl anymore. But I am. I am a girl with short, spiky
hair and carefully grown muscles. I push the lace curtains to the side to let the last bit of light fill my room.
The shadows accent my deltoids and triceps better than
direct sunlight.

I move closer to the mirror. My hair is so short now

that I couldn't hide myself inside it if I wanted to. I'm over hiding. My face survived today—my ribs, not so much. Russell nailed my ribs pretty good.

I take off my T-shirt and unhook my swimsuit top. I'll be purple tomorrow; I'm already tender there, underneath my breast. Since moving to Wren, every part of me has changed. My arms are cut like I've been carved out of stone instead of skin and bones. My skin has browned from swimming in the Sipsey in the afternoons. I am brown all over except for my white breasts and the halter-top outline of my swimsuit. I love how my breasts look.

When I raise my arms above my head, my ribs hurt. Maybe it's the cold air from the ceiling fan or maybe it's seeing myself changed, but my breasts tingle. I brush the inside of my wrists against them and the tingle dances up to my neck, then warms me all the way down. I push my breasts both together; I just barely skim them in a circle with my palm. My pecs are as fine underneath my breasts in the mirror as my apple breasts are; I touch my pecs, too, but nothing happens, nothing warm. I push both my breasts into each other to bring back the nice feeling. My breathing slows down.

My breasts are not a girl's breasts. Mine are ripe and perfect, and I think they are fully grown. Forever, I remember asking Mom if my breasts were done yet and begging her to buy me a padded bra. I wore Mom out always asking if I was filling it in yet. She always answered, "They're coming along. Looking good."

These days, I wear pretty, flowery bras from the ladies' lingerie department and sports bras. I am already a 36C; I suppose they could have grown even more, but I think 36C is just right. I am sure that the 36 is the result of all of my push-ups. My breasts are supported by abnormally large pectoral muscles. That's a benefit of all of my upper-body work.

Mom's upper body looks good, too, especially for her age. She doesn't work out at a gym, but her work in the forest is so physical that she has nicely developed pecs.

I cup my left breast and try patting it to stop the tingling. Then I change my mind and hold both of them extra softly, to bring it back.

This is what makes me a ten and not a three; I am soft and strong in the same places. I turn to the side to look at my breasts from a different angle. With my arms stretched out behind me, I arch my chest up to the ceiling. Arching up makes them fiery, too. I decide right here to give thanks for my breasts every morning and every night for the rest of my life. I commit to doing extra push-ups to keep them both beautiful and strong.

Before Ayma gets to wondering where I am, I put

some dry clothes on and pick up my knitting. I repeat my knitting prayers, adding a new prayer for my breasts: *Thank you for my beautiful, healthy breasts. Keep Dixie and me safe from Russell and Gil. Keep watch over Awanita. Make Delta sweeter, bring Mom and Bud together, and how will I ever belong at school now?*

Finally I go sit on the porch and not talk with Ayma. She is humming to herself, so I listen to her and what's all around me. I hear the cows and think that is enough talking to fill up the air this evening. At the fence line, I see Awanita beside Sue. I think he's getting fat; Sue doesn't like to run with him, but she loves to nurse him. Her bag is full enough that she could probably feed half of the calves out there. With school starting, I have not spent as much time in the field lately. Bud says Awanita is starting to act up and I should probably start watching him more closely. He busted a fence rail the other day; Bud fixed it for me.

I listen to Ayma's needles clacking together while Ayma hums "Eye on the Sparrow." I pick up my knitting and try to find the same rhythm as hers. I speed up to the fastest possible knitting pace I can go without tripping in the yarn. Ayma slows down a bit, and soon we are knitting exactly in time with each other. I stay here a while and try to keep the rhythm with my eyes closed.

I listen. Behind our knitting, the heifers are talking in the field. Behind them is the Black Warrior Forest and all of the sounds that come out of there at this time of night. This is the sound of the forest settling down, or maybe it is the sound of the forest waking up. I do what Bud says to do and try to listen. Right up close, about a million cicadas seem to shout out to me. Behind them, the herd—all tucked in now—lows itself good night. A barred owl calls, *Hoo-hoo-thoo. Who-cooks-for-you?* Ayma cooks for me all the time, I think. My Ayma spot itches. I stop knitting and look at Ayma and remember what she said on the morning Mom left.

You turned into something else entirely.

I listen again for the forest, and everything is quiet. No cicadas or cows; the owl is silent, too. *You turned into something else entirely.*

Am I becoming someone else entirely since I moved to Wren?

CHAPTER TWENTY-SEVEN

DELTA'S PERSISTENT KISSING SOUNDS rake my nerves so badly that I could do two hundred push-ups and still be as peeved as I am right now. Unfortunately for him, Delta's regular bus seat is right behind Dixie and me. This afternoon, he is in the dangerous habit of leaning into our personal space and smacking his lips, singing the stupid, unoriginal K-I-S-S-I-N-G song. Whenever I turn around, he sticks his tongue out, then ducks behind the seat.

For the past few months, Russell and Gil have been faking like they are best buds with Delta on the bus, and egging him on to tell everyone, every day, the story of how Delta found Dixie and me sleeping together in Dixie's bed. We were *sleeping*. Dixie sleeps in a double bed, just like I do. We were sleeping next to each other in Dixie's bed.

Before, in the fourth grade, everything happened fast and for no reason, the same as this. When you are best friends with someone, it means that you love them. It means that you love having them in your life. My best friend before Dixie was Krystal. I loved Krystal; I love Dixie even more.

"Stop it, Delta! Stop being such a chronic brat!" I yell. Dixie snorts and stomps her feet hard in agreement with me. Delta could not care less that I might tell Bud. I regret ever having stuck up for him for even one second that day at the Sipsey River; Delta doesn't even know I defended him. He just insists on being a demonic boy with every breath God gives him. Delta sticks his tongue out again, and this time stepping into the aisle, he does a little booty dance of shaking his tail around in circles. He is daring me, but I ignore him.

I used to never get into fights. Since moving here, fights tend to find me without a lot of effort. Plus, it is no exaggeration that I can now do a variety of one hundred and fifty push-ups with a minimum of effort. I like to mix it up with knuckle, fingertip, and diamond push-ups. When Delta is acting like a normal child, I even do push-ups with him on my back. He never acts like a normal child on the bus.

Every day on the bus, it's the same. Russell and Gil sit in the very back, but they don't sit together. They each sit alone in the two back seats, Russell on the left side and Gil on the right. Dixie and I share our seat, coming and going. Our seat has a big rip down the middle. Dixie sits by the window, and I sit on the aisle. All the girls on our bus sit with the same friend to and from school, every day. So it's not like it's a big deal to sit by Dixie all the time, except that Russell and Gil have taken to calling me "queer" and "funny."

I think they call me those names to be jerks. I sort of wish I had my long hair back because part of me wants to hide. Then I change my mind and ignore them; I would rather be me than either Russell or Gil any day of the week. Why would anybody care so much about hating me or Dixie or anybody else?

Today it's worse because Delta is broadcasting that Dixie and I were spooned in the same bed when I stayed at Bud's. I hate Delta. I can't breathe. I try to push this feeling down, way down, but there is nowhere left for it to go. There is not a centimeter left in me.

Delta sings nonstop now; the others on the bus join in, singing with him. "Dixie and Mary Harold sitting in a tree, K-I-S-S . . ." Dixie's neck stiffens, and her white bug eyes make it clear that she is afraid; she doesn't like what is happening, and neither do I. Mrs. King, our bus driver, yells at everyone to quiet down.

I think about reaching across Dixie and opening our window for air. I try to force the shallow breaths deeper into my chest. I close my eyes, and everything spins, so I open them and look straight ahead.

Delta finishes the song with his booty dance. He is standing right in my face and sticks his tongue out again. This time, he licks his bottom lip slowly. I am so sure he learned that from Russell Cauliflower.

"Big man," I say, "get that tongue back in your mouth and sit down."

He retrieves his tongue, like he is listening this time. Of course it's Delta, so I take a moment to reinforce how serious I am about stopping this nonsense.

"Now, if you stick that milky-fungified tongue out one more time, I am going to smack it down your throat."

Dixie cheers me on with a whinny and a head toss. Everybody else says, "Ooooooooooooh." That makes Delta's face turn red.

Because he truly is an idiot, Delta sticks out his

tongue. Because I have no more room left to push anything else down, I make good on my words. With all of the force of my extraordinary upper-body strength and all of my anger at Delta for being a brat, for killing that chipmunk, at Russell and Gil for being bullies, shoot, I guess even at Mom for not being here, I slam Delta's tongue so swiftly and with such might, that I can feel the film left on his unbrushed teeth. I hit him again, to be sure that he shuts up for good. I hit him once more. And again I hit him, and I truly do wish that I had that shovel and he is lucky that I don't. I probably hit him one or three more times, and when I reach my arm back once more, the person behind me grabs my elbow.

"Stop it. Stop it, Cricket—he's my brother," says a husky voice that I have never heard.

My best, and only, friend, Dixie, stops me. Her voice asks me to stop beating Delta. I lay off Delta, and the bus screeches to a halt, too.

Blood is rushing down Delta's face and he is crying loud. He screams through his tears at Dixie, "Shut up, horse girl! I'm not your brother. You're just a stupid horse. I don't have a sister."

Everyone else on the bus goes completely silent. Mrs. King, who is more endowed with upper-body mass than strength, grabs my sweatshirt by the hood and drags me to the front of the bus. I feel her back arm wings against my cheek. She doesn't call me sweetie or baby.

She hollers at me, "Miss Woods, who do you think you are? Get off of my bus."

And seriously, she opens the door and shoves me out. I think it must be illegal for her to do this, drop a student off at an unauthorized stop on the side of the road. Mrs. King doesn't waste a second more with me.

Standing on the shoulder, I look at my hand, my right hand that hit Delta. My knuckles are bloody, but not bleeding. My right hand is bloody with Delta. I wipe as much Delta off of my hand as I can onto my hoodie. The bus pulls away, and I stand there, bloody and two and a half miles from home.

Russell and Gil are plastered against the back, yelling something foul at me, which I can't hear. I can see from their faces and hands that it is something along the lines of, "Shut down, bitch!" I look for Dixie's face in the window.

I've walked way farther than two and a half miles before; this is not such a big deal to walk home. The whole ride home from school is just a straight shot down Wren Road, then turn right at the sign for the entrance to the Black Warrior Forest. I think I am going to have to tell Mom this time.

CHAPTER TWENTY-EIGHT

THE WALK HOME takes me about an hour because I'm in no hurry and the hill kind of gets me winded. When I'm home, I set my backpack inside the porch and hope that Ayma doesn't see me. From my bag, I dig out the grapes that I always save for Awanita and head to the field to find him. My baby deer will love the grapes.

All of the calves, except Awanita, are huddled together at the fence line with the babysitters. Sue stands grazing at the back, keeping apart from the rest. Awanita, for once, is not nursing. He is nearby, copying his mother. His baby spots are fading; next spring I think he'll have antler buds. I skip over the thought that keeps popping in my mind about Awanita leaving. I know from hanging around forest rangers my whole life that little bucks leave their mamas. Maybe Awanita thinks he's a cow and will live in this pasture instead of the forest.

As I reach the two of them, Awanita lifts his head in my direction to smell the air. He walks to me; his nose is cold and moist. I feel relieved to be here in the field with him. Some of Delta's dried blood is still on my hand. Awanita smells it and runs away. I hold the grapes out, but he keeps his distance now. Usually he gobbles down the grapes, then pushes his head into me, looking for more, but this afternoon we stand for a long time staring at each other.

I drop my head instead of looking right at him; that works with Sue and Dixie. Awanita lifts one leg and holds it there for a long time; he even reaches his neck out toward me, like he wants to come back. He turns away from me and runs to Sue. I know how he feels. I would run to my Mom, too, if I could.

Sue is sweet when she sees me. I lean into her barrel and turn my head flat on top of her. I sync up our breathing until it is exactly the same. I drape my arms across her; I breathe out long and press full into her. I inhale a deep breath until my belly blows out big into

Sue's body. When I exhale again, I try to draw Sue's belly back into my own. Sue stops grazing and stands, not flinching, letting me breathe. I repeat my balloon breaths with Sue until my mind is empty. I breathe out Delta and breathe in Sue. I exhale my achy chest that wants Mom. Then I sink my feet into the ground and inhale the stillness of my cow.

Sue smells so warm. This afternoon, there is a coolness that makes the air finally feel like autumn. Sue's body heats me up from the inside. I move in closer, as close as I can, into her warmth. She lets me breathe with her until Awanita wants to nurse. When he bleats, making his kitty-cat sound, Sue shakes me off and goes to him. I follow her and try to breathe with her again while he nurses. Babies are so greedy; Awanita snorts, kind of like Dixie does sometimes, until I leave the two of them alone. Sue turns fully to her baby deer, licking behind his ears. Neither of them seems at all interested now in whether or not I am here. Late-blooming Queen Anne's lace and goldenrod at the edge of the forest are the only things left over now of summer. I want my mom.

Back home, Mrs. King and the principal have already called Ayma. Bud has already called, too. Ayma sits me down at the kitchen table and gives me the full summary of the situation. She tells me to listen carefully without interrupting to everything she has to tell me. I hide my head in my folded arms and listen to Ayma's report.

Technically the school bus is considered school property, so I am kicked out of school for ten days. The principal thinks I have a propensity for fighting. When I start back to school, I'll get special services from the county to work on my anger and self-control.

I split Delta's lip open when I hit him, and he had to go to Moulton to get it stitched up. Two teeth got knocked out, too, by me hitting him over and over. I guess I busted up Delta pretty badly. I hope Bud is not too mad at me. According to Ayma, he said Delta has had it coming, and if it weren't for me busting on Delta, it likely would've been somebody else. Bud loves Ayma way too much to say anything other than that; that is what I think.

While Ayma tells me precisely how she has heard what I already know, I trace Wren Mountain on the kitchen table. My bloodstained sweatshirt speaks for me. Delta's blood, also splattered across my seashell necklace, confirms what Ayma already knows. I am guilty.

I make the mistake of looking up to see if Ayma is watching me. This is what Ayma wants. She wants this moment, when I look into her eyes.

Ayma holds my eyes to hers and waits for my insides to settle. Her eyes are blue like those birds singing at the

Sipsey River way high above me and Dixie at the end of summer, right before I turned into a bully. Hers are the only set of eyes that I could look into forever, without turning away. Ayma's eyes just suck me right into her. If I could fly away somewhere into Ayma this very instant, I believe everything would be all right. And for a few minutes, maybe everything will be all right.

"You don't know your own strength," she says. "I don't believe, not for half a second, that you meant to hurt that child. But hurt him you did." I still don't look away.

I remember Mom telling me *Do not look into her eyes, do not look into her eyes.* Mom was wrong; you have to look into Ayma's eyes, it's the only way to get right again.

"You know, people are going to talk about you no matter where you live. That's what people do, my beauty. People feel better, more complete, when they find fault with others; it's a way of covering up their own peculiarity." She waits for me to say something.

"Do people talk about you?" I ask, hoping that this is my opening to get the conversation off of me and the school-bus incident.

"If they do, I pay them no mind. You can't. You have to get your heart right, live your life, and love the people around you."

"I guess people must not talk about you too much if

you're not sure or don't know it," I say. I look back down at the table and start tracing the poplar grain again.

"Cricket, you're not the first controversial woman in our family. This might not mean much to you, but I have worn pants my whole life. Wearing pants to church or uptown was shocking in my day. When I married your grandfather, Harold Woods, who was a prince among men, people talked about me because I was Methodist and wouldn't turn Baptist, like him. Now, as you know, many of my good friends are Baptist, but I'm not. Methodist is just as good as Baptist, so I wasn't about to change. When Harold had his first bad stroke, people talked about me because I took care of him up here on Wren Mountain and wouldn't put him in the nursing home in Moulton. These days, it's the folks who do put their people in a home who get talked about. Not too long after he died, I fired the farm manager—we had two hundred head back then—and took over running the entire operation myself."

I can picture all of this about Ayma; some of this story about Ayma and my grandfather I even knew before, like Ayma wearing pants and refusing to turn Baptist, but none of it ever struck me as unusual or different. To me, that's all just Ayma being Ayma. I never thought about these things causing her a problem.

I look up at her face to see if she's watching me. She's not; Ayma's staring off in her own world now. I don't try to find her eyes. I just listen.

"At first, no one in Wren would trade with me. They made excuses about me having no credit of my own and being a high-risk customer. I had to go to Decatur to buy feed or get my tractor fixed. But after a few years of my cows consistently bringing top dollar at Cullman, folk started coming around. One by one, they started to change." Ayma waits for a second, I think, to see if this is enough for me.

I am still stuck in my own scandal; Ayma adds on something about Mom.

"Your mother brought her share of scrutiny our way. Bye was, as you may or may not know, a wild child. People said I was an unfit mother. She got caught buying moonshine over in Winston County, the other side of the forest from us, when she was fifteen. Can you believe it? Because of her, of course, folks have been talking about you since your days in the womb, having no named father."

Ayma doesn't say anything else, and we sit in silence together. I cuddle up to her and think about everything I can remember.

"Did I have pneumonia when I was a little bitty girl?"

"You surely did. We almost lost you." Ayma pats my

back in circles. I love when she does this. "You stayed in the hospital for several weeks."

"Did Mom bring me to Wren to stay for a month so you could take care of me?"

"Don't tell me you remember that, too!"

"I read it in my baby book. 'Took Cricket to Mother's in Wren for one month. Pneumonia.'" I wish that I could remember it because I think Ayma probably loved me back to myself. If I could remember, I bet anything I would remember gazing into Ayma's fair blue eyes and getting lost in them enough to forget about the pneumonia clamping down on my lungs. Maybe it was only when I looked into Ayma that I could breathe. I am certain that if I could, I would remember knowing, even then, when I was too little to have words, that what was in her eyes for me was the very deepest, strongest love that I will ever know.

"I rocked you day and night. You held my hand so tight with your little fingers. You would fall asleep looking right up at me. You have always been precious to me, Cricket. More than a granddaughter, really more like my own."

I slip off my sock and shoe and hold my right foot up for Ayma to see. "Have you ever noticed my big old ugly toe?"

"It's a mark of distinction, that long second toe, and yes, I have. Why do you ask?"

"Did my granddaddy have one? Harold? Did he?"

"No, that sweet man had short, stubby toes. Bye got his feet."

"I have a beauty mark on my calf, Ayma, just like yours. I like knowing I got this mole from you; it kind of makes me feel protected."

Ayma's face lights up, and she pulls me close into her. "You are protected even more than you know, for my own grandmother was marked the way we are. You never knew her, but you have this beautiful part of her."

My long second toe is crooked; there is nothing beautiful about it. I find Ayma's swimming-pool eyes and tread in them.

"I don't miss having a father. Most of the time, I don't know what I would do with one, especially now that I've got Bud around. But this ugly toe came from somewhere, didn't it?"

Ayma blinks and smiles. She takes a deep breath like she is thinking of something good to say. I save her from having to be all wise.

"Ayma, will she ever name my father?"

"Bye might be the most peculiar of us all, Cricket. I can't answer your question, precious. I wish I could."

She lets this sink in for a second. Then Ayma tells me, "By the way, your mama wants you to call her."

Ayma sees my panic starting and assures me, "I didn't say a word about any of this business with Delta. That's for you to handle."

"Yes, ma'am." I nod. Then I start for the kitchen, to call Mom.

Ayma reaches out for my hand and pats me. The swimming pools have won. I look directly at her, and without making a sound, I start sobbing all over the outline of Wren Mountain on the kitchen table.

"My beauty," she offers, "as far as you and Dixie, or you being funny, as they like to say—well, love between two females, whatever kind of love it is, still makes people come undone. It always does. People talk. You and Dixie love each other; be thankful you found her and she you."

I look into her face, hoping her blue eyes will make me feel better without me having to speak a word, like *I'm sorry* or *I didn't mean to* or *please forgive me*. I try to say something to Ayma, but every sound I make comes out a tear. Her eyes are holding me in this place of being unable to move or speak, but just able only to look at Ayma—with her hair cut boyish like mine and telling me she is more controversial than I am because she wears pants, and I am believing every word she tells me because she has lived here for a long time and lived exactly, just exactly, how she has wanted to live.

While I cry on Wren Mountain, I think about all of the other knitters, the same ladies who insisted on telling me the correct way to wipe when I first got here. They are also the same ladies who told me about their children who were never born and the hardships they had bringing out the ones who were born. These very same ladies still wear skirts, not pants; they get permanent waves in their hair at the beauty parlor every week. Ayma is different, just like me and just like Mom.

Once I am all emptied out, Ayma rubs my back like I guess she has been doing forever.

"Cricket," she tells me, "time to face yourself and call Bye."

I trace Wren Mountain with my pointer finger. I wish Mom were here so I could explain the truth face-to-face.

Chapter Twenty-nine

BEFORE I CAN CALL HER, Mom calls me. I figure that Bud must have gotten to her first, so I blurt out the full story to get my side completely out. I tell Mom that Delta is a wicked boy; she won't listen. I am grounded for eternity, or at least until Mom says so — no phone, no TV, no computer, no Dixie. In fact, I cannot see Dixie at all.

"Mary Harold Woods, I hope you are deeply ashamed of yourself. Beating up a defenseless child is not the same thing as kicking a bully's ass to protect someone else," she says.

Again, I repeat the entire story, how it is not all my fault. "First of all, I did not beat him up. I smacked him and —"

Mom interrupts me, "For Christ's sake, you busted his lip open and knocked his two front teeth out. You beat him up. You bullied him. Delta is tiny. You are a very strong, very big girl. You hurt him badly, whether you meant to or not."

"You met Delta. Mom, he is a chronic brat. He wouldn't shut up, calling me queer. He wouldn't shut up. I needed for him to shut up."

"Oh, no. You're not playing that game in Wren."

"You're saying it doesn't matter what people say about me," I complain.

Mom says nothing.

"You're saying you don't care what people say about me," I repeat.

"Right. I do not care what people say about you because you are you and I love you. I love who you are. Queer, not queer, it makes no difference to me."

"Mom, please." I want to tell her that's not the point; she's not listening. I'm tired of being called anything. I just want to be Cricket for once—that's all.

"Cricket, you are free to be yourself in Wren."

Delta's bloody, crying face takes over my mind. I swear, I only wanted to shut him up.

My chest hurts. "I'm afraid of dying," I whisper into

the phone. I think of Awanita and I find a small breath, so I hold on and think only of my deer and cow. I try to breathe deep, like I do in the field with Sue.

"You get to decide who you are. Every day you get to decide. So who are you?" Mom stops talking, waiting for me to be moved to answer.

I close my eyes so I can see her face in my mind.

She asks me again, "Cricket, who are you?"

I am worn out. The Holy Spirit makes me tell her the truth.

I decide to unpack everything I've been carrying inside.

"I am your daughter, Mom—that's who. I am your daughter, and I can't stand being away from you any longer."

"Shhh. Oh, sugar, I'm coming to Wren. Don't worry, I'm coming to Wren."

I wish that she could hold me. "To get me?" I choke out. "You're coming to Wren to get me?

"No, Cricket. I'm coming to Wren to live," Mom says.

My tears hiccup while my crying stops, then starts again for the opposite reason. I need her to say it again. "What?" I cry. "Did you get the job?" I sob louder, and each new wave is bringing me some good relief.

"Maybe — I won't know for another week or so."

"Are you coming back to marry Bud?" I ask in between hiccups.

Mom laughs. "I do not have any plans to marry Bud. I might date him. I haven't decided."

"What? Why are you coming back then?" Truthfully, I don't really care what her reason is. Whether it's Bud or a job, I just need to be with her.

"Sweetest," she tells me, "I am coming to Wren for you. That's all. I am empty and restless without you. More than a forest, or a river, or a tree, and more than myself, I want to protect you. I am coming home to Wren; that's why I called."

"Really?" I ask. My breath is stuttering with tears. I feel another round coming up, but these are different, and I won't push them back down.

"Cricket, I knew when I left you there this summer that I would be back. I had to take care of things first. I've sold the Rattlesnake Creek property to the city. I closed on the house yesterday. Hopefully, the Black Warrior job will work out. If not, I'll do something else. Bud and I have been talking and e-mailing, but we're going to take our time. I am coming home to be with you."

I can't say one word because all of these tears are unpacked now, and I am not about to put them back.

CHAPTER THIRTY

NOW THAT MOM IS HOME, this is our second official hen party, so it's like a welcome-home party for Mom. Everyone is at knitting circle tonight, except for Bud. The ladies are giving Mom extra help and attention, since she's knitting with us for the first time. Mom seems to be trying extra hard to join in and has set out drinks and snacks for the knitters. Ayma keeps a full pantry and freezer, so tonight, there is plenty of already-made food to serve, including cheese straws, my favorite snack of all time.

Knitting circle is not the same without Bud. Because he is home taking care of Delta, we are all adding an extra knitting prayer for Bud. Delta gets a knitting prayer, too. The ladies are all talking and telling funny stories about the week. They all miss Bud, but since he is not here, they are bombarding Mom with questions about whether she and Bud might get back together one day. For good measure, they're also asking if she got the Black Warrior job; the real interest, though, is Mom's love life. None of them have mentioned the Delta incident to me, for which I am grateful enough to add an additional knitting prayer of thanks.

The demand for Bud's campaign scarves is great, almost too great for the knitting circle to handle. In order to boost our production, all of us are using the big needles—the seventeens—and thick yarn now. I am starting a new scarf, and like always, each stitch represents a prayer. I cast on twelve prayers, and one to grow on, that I will send up over and over as the scarf gets longer:

1. Thank you for bringing Mom back to Wren.
2. Bless Bud and everything he has on his shoulders.
3. Forgive me for hurting Delta so badly.
4. I hope Delta gets better and also nicer.
5. Thank you for the knitters not asking me why I beat up Delta.

6. Thank you for my new strength to stick up for Dixie and myself.

7. Please don't let Dixie be mad at me for busting up Delta.

8. Please let Bud win the election and then maybe he will shut up about freaking Thomas Jefferson.

9. Keep it up with Mom and Bud.

10. Please let Mom get the job in the Black Warrior Forest.

11. Please let Hoss bring top dollar at Cullman tomorrow.

12. And, also, let everything work out for Hoss, too — if you know what I mean, Lord, so he's not scared or anything.

13. Please help me not get so angry.

Amen.

Chapter Thirty-one

THE DRIVE TO CULLMAN feels extra long because Bud and I don't talk much. I mean, we say hello and he doesn't seem real perturbed, but I mostly keep to myself. I want to ask about Delta. Even more, I want to tell Bud that Dixie spoke words to me on the bus. I have kept this all to myself. Granted, I was busting on her brother at the time, but I heard Dixie speak with both of my ears: "Stop it, Cricket." I know I am not imagining that; Dixie's words to me are burned into my mind.

In my head, I plan out every sentence that I should be saying right now to Bud, but I cannot get my mouth to cooperate. It just won't do it; it just won't.

Bud, for his part, is trying to go easy on me, though I don't know why. He has already pointed out one wild turkey on the side of the road and commented on every new or newly closed store along the way. Every now and then, I look back to see how Hoss is doing in the trailer; he seems okay to me. He doesn't look scared at all. I tell him with my heart-words that everything will be okay and I hope that is the honest-to-God truth.

I spot the auction house right away because they fly an Old Glory bigger than any I've ever seen, even bigger than at the car dealership we pass on 72 in Decatur. Bud's the one who calls the flag Old Glory. He tips his cap to her when we walk by, as if we were passing a lady in town.

The whiteboard outside lists today's sale and the number of head to be auctioned off. We get up here early so we can do a walk-through before the actual bidding starts. Bud and I have two goals today: one, to sell Hoss, and two, to buy a new bull.

Bud has great patience in the field and will give any animal a fighting chance to thrive in our herd. But Hoss is badly crippled now and, after three rounds of antibiotics, appears no better at all. That lame foot keeps Hoss in a great deal of pain and has rendered him unable to complete his job. The heifers run away from him when he tries to mount. He's about given up trying with the cows because they have taken to kicking his butt.

We've decided to replace him; we are definitely selling Hoss today. I will miss him in a way. He's a good-looking bull, and I have been pulling for him all along.

Disregarding the fact that Hoss is lame and sick, Bud thinks we need a new bull that's a better fit with our herd. Finding the right bull is tricky, not only because we need to keep a good blend of lean muscle to fat but also because we like our herd to be fairly docile and easygoing—not sporty, as Bud would say. Sporty heifers and bulls sometimes step across the leadership line over into troublemaking. A sporty bull is just asking for trouble. I suspect that if I were a heifer, I'd be considered sporty.

Though the Internet is reporting a high sales price of eighty-nine cents per pound at Cullman this week, we'll be happy to get fifty cents a pound for Hoss. We probably won't even get a thousand dollars for him total, with his bad foot and untreatable infection. Hoss will go up for auction with the other breakers.

Breakers are cattle that are too old to calve any longer or those who, like Hoss, are sick or injured beyond the point of full or affordable recovery. No matter what the high price is for cattle, the breakers go for way less than top-dollar.

No matter how long it takes, the Cullman Livestock Auction will last until every one of these one thousand three hundred five head sells. Some folks here, like us, are looking to pick up a good bull or some new heifers. Others, also like us, are here to unload their breakers.

Before we sit down to watch the auction, Bud and I walk behind the auctioneer's stand to see if we might find the right bull to take home. Most of the viewing is done from a catwalk high above the labyrinth of chutes packed full with cows. If we spot something with potential, we can go down below and have a closer look.

I watch the lots of breakers—Angus, Charolais, Hereford, even a few Holsteins, typically a dairy cow, are here. I see several lots of heifers and steers who must have just been weaned because they are bleating so loudly. These don't look like calves anymore, but you can tell they are still babies inside themselves, hollering for their mamas.

Sue was a breaker when Bud bought her for me; now she is one of our best cows.

Bud is busy inspecting the bulls. I elbow him to get

his attention. "Hey, I don't want Sue to ever come here again. Okay?"

Bud just nods and answers me with his own question. "What do you think of that little bull right there? He's good-looking, huh?" He points to a young Black Angus, a little smaller than Sue. He's big enough to get the job done, but not yet full grown.

I nod my agreement that this bull is good-looking, but keep thinking about Sue and Awanita. I am worried that Awanita is getting too rambunctious for the herd. Same way that Bud reasons acceptance about Sue's calf dying, he cites acceptance about the probability of Awanita leaving the herd, too. Bud is not the least bit concerned about the baby deer; he says it will all work out like it's supposed to.

Someday, after Bud and I have healed over from all this with me busting Delta, we are going to have to talk about how hard it is raising cattle. Like now, I have gone and gotten attached to Number Forty-eight and she doesn't even have her own name; she's only got a number. She finally had that calf of hers. Even though her bag is still not right, the calf is working it out and demanding to live and be healthy. I'm going to break up into pieces when we sell the calf next year and whenever we sell Number Forty-eight. Just because she doesn't have a name doesn't mean I won't come to love her almost like I do Sue.

As the black bull that we're watching winds his way through the chute-maze toward the auction house, Bud and I head inside to claim a seat on the front row. I am one of a handful of girls or women here. I'd guess the ratio is about fifteen to one, male to female. But that doesn't bother me. For one, even with my perfect breasts, most people don't immediately recognize that I'm a girl when I'm wearing my working clothes. For two, Bud and I both are wearing *Hale Yes!* caps, and I look like I belong with Bud. Some of these guys, Bud for one, come up here enough that the auctioneer knows them and remembers their special sign for bidding.

We see the little Angus bull come up for bid, and right away I can tell, by the auctioneer's gestures, that we've got heavy competition with someone up in the stands directly behind us and another one to our right, a few rows back. Bud holds off on bidding right away and lets the field shake out a bit to see if we'll get a chance. When the bidding nearly stalls at eighty-five cents a pound, Bud dives in so quick that nobody notices but the auctioneer.

Bud's sign is almost prayerful. He bows his head, clasps his hands together, and raises his right index finger. That's the beauty of Bud. He gets the little bull for eighty-six cents a pound. We'll pay a little shy of eight hundred dollars for him. Once he's done bidding, Bud yanks his cap off and runs his hand through his hair, then puts his cap back on his head.

Bud does fast math in his head and says to me, "We're going to have to get forty-nine for Hoss," meaning that forty-nine cents per pound is our break-even point.

When Hoss comes into the auction house, Bud and I leave our seats and stand in the hall, where we can see the auction board, but not Hoss or the bidding. I feel bad leaving Hoss alone in the auction house, but I'm also relieved not to have to see him standing there with people who I know are bidding to kill him. I watch the board; Bud listens to the auctioneer. His head is down in bidding position. On his left side Bud looks relaxed, with his hand tucked into his jeans. His right side is tensed up from his shoulder to his fist as he waits to hear the final bid. I see the board post forty-three at the same time Bud hears it. "Damn. Well, at least we didn't lose our pants." That's Bud-speak for *It could have been worse.*

We hustle to load our new bull quickly and set home for Wren. Bud is ticked about losing money on Hoss. I look around for Hoss; I want to see him just to say good-bye or to remind him to be brave. Bud says there's no time for good-bye. I have to let Hoss go; we have a new bull now. I glance back at the little Angus bull, and he looks scared.

I planned to apologize to Bud this morning on the way to Cullman. Since we first started out this morning, I have been trying to persuade myself to come out and say *sorry* about Delta. On the way home, Bud wants to talk about the civility of political life in T.J.'s day, as compared to modern times. Bud's so sure about this that I can't bring myself to tell him that Thomas Jefferson was kind of a back-stabber to John Adams. Due to Mr. Beckett saying ugly things about Bud's morals in an interview with the *Lawrence County Bulletin,* he is particularly sensitive these days. The Beckett campaign has started sending around flyers about Bud's children living in a broken home. For the duration of the ride home, Bud talks about how ugly the race is this year.

I rehearse my Delta apology in my mind. I keep rehearsing until Bud drops me off at home. At the last minute, I chicken out and only manage to say, "See you later at knitting? I'll try to fix the gate tomorrow." Then I jump out of the truck.

Bud looks as though he's waiting for me to say what I've been intending to say all morning. He waits for my apology. After a few seconds, though, he lets it go. "I'll leave you a list for tomorrow, champ. If you would try to fix that gate that your little deer mangled first, I'd appreciate it." Awanita is not winning himself any friends here lately with his acting up. If Awanita weren't a deer, he'd be taken to Cullman for being sporty.

Chapter Thirty-two

TONIGHT IS OUR LAST CHANCE to knit up campaign scarves for Bud. With less than a week to go before the election, we added an extra knitting circle to knit up another forty or fifty *Hale Yes!* scarves.

Our circle is happy to help Bud out; we all think he is going to win big this year, finally. Tonight extra ladies have arrived to lend a hand. Twenty knitters have crammed into our house, planning to finish as many scarves as we can over the next four hours. I think I can get two done if I don't talk too much or get distracted.

Louisa is not here because she has pneumonia and is in the hospital. We all add a prayer stitch for her. Almost all of the ladies have battled pneumonia before, so they are enjoying telling their own pneumonia stories. Madilee does not have a pneumonia story, but she does have a congestive heart failure story, and that is good enough. Even I have a pneumonia story; the one from when I was a baby and Ayma took care of me. Turns out the knitters remember my story because most of them came up here to Wren Mountain and visited me back then.

"You were such a sweet little thing, sweet as you could be. I don't believe your grandmother has ever uttered a sentence without your name in it, Mary Harold," says Madilee. "That's how sweet you are." She pats my leg when she calls me sweet.

They all know that I beat up Delta, and that I've been suspended twice now for fighting. Could be that all of this "I'm so sweet" business is just knitters' reverse psychology to get me to act sweet. Or it could be that I am sweet and tough all rolled into one girl. I prefer to think that I'm sweet and tough.

I'm surprised when Bud actually shows up after being in Cullman all day. I thought he'd be staying home with Delta. The ladies cheer and start chanting, "Hale, Yes! Hale, Yes! Hale, Yes!" Even Mom joins in the chant until finally, they all bust up laughing and hooting and hugging Bud. He thanks the ladies for their hard work on the scarves and their solid belief in his campaign.

Once the knitting ladies settle down from the excitement of Bud's arrival, I see Delta hiding behind his dad. I wish I could rewind the past a couple of weeks and get back to right before I pummeled him on the bus. I made a choice when I beat Delta. Not so much a choice to hurt him as bad as I did, but a choice to make him stop. Looking back, maybe there was another choice waiting for me. I didn't listen for it, the way Ayma and Bud, and even Mom, keep showing me how to do. In the second that I had not to sock him, I could have tried something else. Maybe Bud was right that being gentle can be just as strong as being forceful.

Maybe Delta would have shut up if I had started singing the K-I-S-S-I-N-G song with him. Or I could have pulled his hoodie up over his head and tied it so tight that he only had a tiny hole available for breathing. It would have been hilarious and effective to watch Delta bumping around on the bus trying to find his way back to his seat. Or, he's so little, I could have easily pinned him down and tickled his armpits until he laughed so hard that he could no longer sing, stick his tongue out, or shake his tail at me. I did not want to hurt Delta.

Okay, that's a lie. I wanted to hurt him, all right. I had been imagining cutting him in half with that shovel, just like he did to the chipmunk. Now that I have hurt him this badly, I take it back, only it's too late to come undone. That's what I really wanted on the bus; I wanted everything to come undone.

When I look at Delta standing there with Bud in the doorway, Delta waves his hand at me once and then turns away from me. His lip is still swollen, and I can see the little black stitches keeping it together.

Bud walks over to me and says, "Scrapper! How's it going?" This is the first time Bud has said anything directly to me about my beating Delta. He is trying to be cool about the fact that I creamed his son.

"Good, it's going good. I'm sorry about Delta, Bud," I finally say.

"All right, but you ought to tell that to Delta, huh? He'll be fine. He's a tough customer." He calls for Delta to come over, "Hey, champ! Come on over here. Mary Harold wants to talk to you, and she's going to get you started knitting."

I conquer my impulse to tell Bud that I will not be helping Delta cast on because he is still a brat.

Delta comes over and right away complains about having to knit. "I'm not knitting. I'm only here because you made me come see her." He points to me.

"Son," Bud says to Delta, "I need you to help me out. We're real close this year—I can feel it. We're going to win."

"You say that every time and we never win," Delta whines back.

I am trying hard to apologize to Delta.

Mom sees me struggling to keep breathing; she comes to help me. "Mary Harold? Did you want to say something to Delta?"

I feel her hand in my back, right above my butt. "I did. I mean, I do." I kneel down to Delta and look him in the eyes.

His eyes are blue, too. I would have sworn they were brown. They are not nearly as comforting as Ayma's swimming pools, but they are a sweet, little-boy blue. I really thought they were brown.

"Delta, I am sorry that I knocked your teeth out." I stop myself from adding, *If you hadn't been acting like an idiot, you could have avoided the pain altogether.*

He nods and flicks two false teeth at me. "I got false teeth to replace the ones you knocked out. Ain't that cool?" He flicks, again.

"Put your teeth back in your mouth, son. Now, let Mary Harold teach you how to knit," Bud orders Delta.

Delta is using smaller-size needles, but we are still letting him knit up a scarf so he can be a contributor to the effort. His scarf will look different from all the others, but I tell Delta that means that his will be more valuable when Bud wins. Mom especially dotes on Delta at knitting circle, telling him she hopes he will knit her a scarf one day. Delta gets bashful-looking when she does that and shrinks up into the sofa cushions. Mom is of the opinion that all Delta needs is positive attention to straighten out. Personally, I am not so sure that will do the trick. I think the child probably needs as many special services as the county has to offer.

I tell Delta about how when we cast on each stitch, we are actually casting on a special wish or prayer that goes directly to God from the knitter. He flicks his teeth while he is thinking about this idea. I go to the kitchen and eat some cheese straws while Delta thinks and flicks.

"Okay, I'm ready," he tells me when I get back.

I assure the devil-child that although I'm the one doing the casting, the prayers are his. Delta nods and flicks. Mom and Bud are over there pretending they don't hear us.

Then, Delta tells me: "Number one: Let Bud win the election. Number two: Tell Mary Harold not to beat on me anymore. Number three: I'm sorry that I killed that chipmunk; the girls were leaving me out like they always do. Number four: Turn Dixie back into my sister. And five—"

Delta flicks the teeth again.

"Go ahead; it's okay. God wants to know what number five is," I say.

"Number five: Me and Dixie could use a new mama."

He's so businesslike when he says number five. He gives me a quick, sharp little nod like he's all done. I never have had a moment of truly liking Delta, really. I have to admit that none of Delta's prayers except for number two are selfish. I decide I will think about possibly giving Delta a second chance.

Delta can't get the hang of knitting. His hands aren't used to such small, fine movements, and he loses his patience over and over. I've got him using size eleven needles, smaller than the seventeens that the rest of us use, thinking those might be more his size.

Like me, when I was learning to knit, Delta doesn't see the yarn the right way at first. He picks up stitches in the wrong place and mostly ends up adding three or four extra on every row, or dropping a few because they slip off before his fingers can remember the proper motion. So far, his work is uneven and lumpy; that makes him mad.

When Delta makes another knitting mistake, he throws his needles on the floor. "This is stupid. I don't have to do this."

Since I have been forced into being his knitting

buddy, I give him a pep talk. "Stop being a baby, Delta. Pick up your knitting and fix it," I say.

Instead of sticking his tongue out at me now, he flashes his fake, temporary teeth. He loves those teeth.

"I'm not being a baby," Delta whimpers. "I can't do it. The prayers won't stay on. I want the prayers to stay on." Delta begins to cry.

If the ladies, or anybody, notices, they pay no mind.

"The prayers won't stay on," he says again.

"Here." I take his knitting from him. "Watch."

This time I teach him the rhyme that Ayma taught me. "In through the front door, run around back, peep through the window, off jumps Jack. Watch again." I demonstrate slowly. "Now you try it," I say.

One step at a time, Delta matches his hands to the verse. He knits a whole row without dropping a stitch.

"Delta," I tell him, "the prayers don't ever fall off, even if the yarn does."

He nods and flicks.

Chapter Thirty-three

AFTER KNITTING, I walk Delta home to Bud's because he's too tired to keep his eyes open any longer. Mom and Bud keep playing like they are not dating. We all know the real deal; they are getting pretty tight. Delta is light as a leaf, so I piggyback him most of the way across the field to Bud's. He rests his cheek on my shoulder, and I let him put his head down on me without a hassle. I think it took a lot out of him to knit, especially to add that prayer for a new mama. By the time I get him to Bud's house, Delta has fallen asleep.

I just tuck him on the den sofa without waking Dixie, because technically my groundation is still in effect. I set him down and pull a blanket up over him so he won't get too cold. All this time, Delta has been wanting his sister back or a new mama.

All this time, Delta acted so evil. Could he really just be needing the same things I've been needing? Maybe so.

While he's sleeping, I tell Delta again, "I'm sorry, Delta, about busting you up. I'm real sorry."

In case he can kind of hear me, like I can sometimes kind of hear Mom, I bend over and kiss his forehead, same way she does me. I kiss him like a mama would, then I slip out the door as quickly as I can.

I am comfortable walking home through the pasture alone. I mean, it's not exactly like I'm walking through the woods. On the edges, I am surrounded by forest since basically Ayma's place is a six-hundred-acre slice of fields cut from the Black Warrior.

Bud's herd and our herd are quiet and invisible tonight. None of them is lowing; they all must be settled at the tree line near the forest. I like knowing that the cows, and Awanita, are just across the road.

The driveway is empty when I get home. Bud's not even standing around on the porch. Mom and Ayma are clearing dishes in the dining room; I pass on by them and holler in, "G'night, y'all. Love you!"

"Love you!" they both call back, and Mom adds, "I'll come up in a bit."

I know she'll forget or I'll be asleep when she remembers.

Even though it's cold out, I raise my bedroom window — the one closest to Awanita and the Black Warrior. I want to be near them all night.

Through the open window, the late-October air brings a fast sleep to me — a sleep that starts out dark like the night, with no moon, only still air. When I have slept enough, I step out of the window and into the forest alone, without Mom or Dixie. A silvery ribbon binds me to my sleeping self, and I have no fear of how I'll get home when I am ready to return. I sit down on a boulder and take off my shoes and socks, leaving them on the rock. The forest floor is covered with leaves, though there are still thousands of yellow leaves twinkling on the poplar branches above me. I burrow myself down until I feel the hot earth on my face and my bare feet.

Deep in the canyon stands Sophia; she did not fall — that was only a dream. I hear water falling and laughter rising. I walk to the flat rock edge of the pool. I sit and begin washing my feet. The water is so cold at first that my breath swirls around and around in my chest like a shallow eddy in the Sipsey, until it finds a pathway out. The invisible laughing gets louder. I soak up the hidden laughter.

I close my eyes and think back over the last few months. So much has changed, and so much has stayed the same. I recall our knitting prayers. One by one I speak my prayers and Delta's prayers aloud. The laughing stops while I pray for Delta and for myself. Though I can see no one else around, I speak the prayers loudly and clearly because I want these prayers to be heard by God and God's earth. Then I wait long enough for the Holy Spirit to have heard the prayers, too. I leave the prayers here at the waterfall in the forest. We will cast new ones when we come together again.

I feel a sweet, wet nose on my cheek; I open my eyes. Awanita grunts and kisses my face. Old friends now, we exchange breaths. The deer doesn't linger or even give me a good-bye sniff. He leaves me to myself. I stretch out full and imagine the day I will see him again, when he is a grown buck.

The water and laughter that were a moment ago hidden behind a veil now reveal everyone waiting for me. The Indian girl of my dream who first guided me to Awanita stands under the spray, in water up to her bare shoulders. Ayma is with her, only her hair is dark and long, tied back with a lavender ribbon. She is smiling and giggling, like a girl. Ayma floats on her back, and the Indian holds her in the water, like Mom held me when I was little and just learning to swim. Dixie and Mom float with them, too, the three of them holding on to one another's hands, making a float-star in the water.

I wave and wonder how Ayma made it all the way out here into the canyon. I wonder if I should take her back home. She looks strong. Ayma knows the forest well; this is her home, like it is Mom's and Dixie's. Ayma bobs up and smiles; she calls me into the water. A breeze blows around my face, wrapping me up and pulling me in.

I close my eyes to breathe everything in deep: the breeze, the laughter, the warmth from the earth, and the golden poplar halo. I step out of my clothes and I am by myself. Ayma, Dixie, and Mom have vanished. The Indian stands on the flat rock beside Awanita, watching me, ready to leave.

Wait—who are you?

This time, she doesn't run away or turn from me when I call to her. She opens herself to the forest around us—our forest, the Black Warrior Forest, where her people, my people, and all of our people have lived since any of us can remember and since any of us have been writing it all down.

This girl, she might have been there in the first forest. The Sipsey River was here curling through the foothills, slowly making canyons deeper over the centuries while the men were fighting about what the land should be called and who should get to live or die on it.

Someday this place will be a canyon even grander than the one in Arizona. The Great Sipsey Canyon will be the opposite of the red canyon. Our canyon will be green and blue with luscious mossy rock offering respite for anyone who needs it. Anyone who needs to find out where they belong can come into the Sipsey and here they will find an oasis instead of a dry desert. They'll find an entire world of hidden ancestors and guides—some who can be found in the forest, others who can be found within. Maybe, like me, they'll find their home.

The girl and my deer turn to leave. She hasn't answered my question.

Who are you?

Like she did on the last day of June, when I dreamed her the very first time, the girl gives me one word. She touches her hand to her heart and speaks to me in my language. *"Hope,"* she says. "I am Hope."

Chapter Thirty-four

TODAY I AM TOTALLY ON MY OWN. Bud has taken Dixie and Delta to the Wren Indian Festival, where they are all three a part of the official activities. Mom wouldn't even let me off groundation to go with them. It has been a week and a half now, and I have seen Dixie exactly once since she called my name on the bus. Besides the fact that I miss her and want to make things right between us, I could use her help getting all of these cows back home.

I thought was only going to be fixing the gate that Awanita wrecked with his crazy bouncing around. I sure didn't count on Awanita and the bull causing the whole herd to escape down the road.

That new bull that we bought in Cullman has been acting so sporty toward my baby deer that we separated them. Even a fence between them didn't work. While I was working on the gate, Awanita got the bull in a tizzy. The bull started ramming the fence and wouldn't quit; he wanted to get at Awanita.

The fence held fine, but only because that new bull is still smallish. Then the whole entire herd freaked out and came charging toward me! I hopped right into the bull's field rather than get mowed down by seventy-four cows and a sporty little buck.

There was nothing I could do to stop the herd once they broke out. The gals basically stampeded and started trotting down the road; they ended up at the cemetery way at the end of our road, most likely because no one has cut the grass there for so long.

The saving grace of my predicament is that the new bull is in a field by himself, and I will not have to face him down in the open graveyard. The downer is that we had just moved every last one of the cows, heifers, and calves together into one field, so they *all* got out. Thankfully, they didn't set off toward the forest, or Ayma would have had my hide.

By their nature, cows are obedient animals; what I call push-button. I know, from working with Bud and watching the herd, which buttons I need to push to walk them all home.

A bucket of grain should do the trick to get the gals moving back down the road. Usually Bud or I enter the field rattling a grain bucket; we know that one cow's leadership is all it takes to get the others to fall in line. The sight of a white bucket is more or less the equivalent of that green flag that starts the NASCAR races. These girls see a white bucket, and they come racing for home because they know there'll be plenty of grain waiting for the winner.

In our fields, narrow cow trails crisscross the grass and the earth is forever worn down and packed firm. These trails work like cow sidewalks, and the girls faithfully use them day in and day out.

There is no worn cow trail here in the cemetery. I am hoping that they are bucket-broke enough to come home with me, when I wave the white bucket and hold out the promise of grain to the first one through the gate, about half a mile down the road.

I only need a single cow.

I stand shaking my bucket, calling them all home.

Sue comes over first. I give her a whiff of the feed and hold out a little taste in my hand. She takes a few steps toward me and then stops to call Awanita. My deer doesn't even look up when Sue calls him. Sue lows again, asking him to join her.

I start walking home slowly, and soon they all follow—all except Awanita. He stays in the cemetery grazing alone. I want to round him up, too, but I can't risk the herd to go chasing Awanita. How would I tell Ayma that my baby deer made me lose seventy-four cows?

I leave him be for now. I count my seventy-four head, which is right. Including the new bull and Awanita, we have seventy-six, so I can account for all of them. With Sue at the front and me holding a bucket that pledges a better-tasting meal than graveyard grass and dandelions, the bunch of us walk, in single file, down the road, through the gate back to our farm. Because of Sue's high position in the herd and her trust of me, I lead them home with ease.

After we're home, I put out extra grain and a new salt lick and do my best to mend the gate that Awanita and the herd wrecked. I feel proud that I rescued the cows by myself. All are home except Awanita, who, for the first time since I found him, is alone.

Once the cows are safe, my worry turns back to Awanita. He is still too young to be out in the forest by himself. He has spent his whole life with cows and people; he's not ready to go. I'm not ready for him to go, either. We didn't even get to say good-bye.

I need Dixie to help me find the deer. I run home to plead with Mom to release me from groundation.

Mom is standing in the driveway, leaning against Bud's truck, tossing her head around while she talks to him, even though her hair is too short to get the full effect. *Good,* I think, *Bud's back from the Indian Festival.* That means Dixie is home, too. I would normally pretend I didn't see Mom and Bud flirting and go about my business, but this is urgent.

"Mom," I interrupt, "Awanita got loose. I need to find Dixie." I don't explain that the entire herd got loose; I can't get into that right now. I urge her, "Please. I know I'm grounded, but Dixie is the only one who knows him like I do."

Bud answers, instead of Mom. "Dixie took off into the forest as soon as we got back, just a little bit ago. She's probably walking the Old Town Path. You could catch her, I bet."

Mom goes right along with Bud. "Okay, go on," she agrees. "Don't get lost."

I look at the two of them, waiting for them to remember that I'm not like everybody else on Wren Mountain. "Umm,

I've never been in the forest alone. Usually Mom, or Dixie, takes me. Are there blazes to follow? I like blazes," I say. Right now is not the time for me to go off into the forest without blazes. I can be Miss Nature Girl later.

Bud chuckles at me. "Champ, you're a natural with the cows, I'll give you that much. We've got some work to do in the forest, though. Tell you what, for hundreds of years folks before us traded and traveled on the Old Town Path. No blazes necessary—enough horses and people have used that path to get to what is now Memphis that you could find your way by the moon if you needed to."

They aren't hearing me; I can't get to the Old Town Path. Besides, the moon's not up yet. I need to find my way in the sunshine. Mom sees that I still need help. She finally gives me directions. "Cut through the back field, and go around the blackberry thicket to the right. You'll see a narrow path there; follow it for about a quarter of a mile into the forest until you come to the marker tree. You can't miss that; it's an old oak tree—about two hundred fifty years old—bent to ninety degrees. Turn with the bend in the tree. Then you're on the Old Town Path."

I take off for the path, and Bud yells some encouragement to me: "Dixie's in there somewhere, for sure."

I turn back to look at them standing there, and I realize now that there is something more than flirting going on between them. I think back to my birthday party, when Bud said he could find me an Indian ancestor for sure. I remember how Ayma made him hush his mouth at the dinner table. I loved Bud's story about the day he and Mom got lost in the forest, the one that made Mom stiffen up and blush like crazy before it made her smile. They were deep in the forest together about a year before I was born: oh, wow. Bud and Mom *know* each other for real.

Mom's pain of not wanting to come back here makes sense to me. She must have loved him for a very long time. I guess he has loved someone else — Starlett. He even made two children with her. Now, that is a real double shot of suck for Mom. I mean Dixie is my best friend, but from Mom's view, that would hurt, all right.

I run back over to Bud and Mom. My hair is the color of his, but my skin is fairer, like Mom's. I am tall like Bud; I tower over Mom and Ayma. I have my precious Ayma spot on my left leg that I wouldn't trade for anything in the world because that spot has got me through everything I have faced so far in my life. I have new strength inside and out that I've grown since being here working on this farm alongside Bud.

"Show me your right foot, Bud." I am grinning like crazy because I know what will be there. I start ripping my own shoe and sock off.

"Hold on, champ." Bud puts his hand on Mom for balance and says to her, "You know I must be seriously charmed by this girl if I'm actually gon' stand here half-barefooted for her."

Mom laughs at him and holds on to his shoulder so he won't fall down.

I wonder if she has figured out yet that I know that right now this is the moment that we will become a family. I put my right foot down in the grass. There's that darned malformed second toe, glaring at all the others. "Set your foot down beside mine."

Bud sees exactly what I see. "Well, I'll be Johnny. You got yourself a toe as ugly as mine. On the right foot, too." He cuts his eyes over to Mom.

She buries her head in Bud's shoulder. "Shh, don't cry." He kisses her hair and then opens his other arm to me. "Come here."

On the very top of Wren Mountain, I hold on to Mom and Bud, and I never want to let them go. Inside myself, I whisper one word that I heard in a dream. *Hope.* Then I get brave and speak it out loud: *"Hope."* Because the girl was right; that's what I found here and on Wren Mountain.

Chapter Thirty-five

THE FIRST PART of getting to the Old Town Path is easy; I know our fields well, and the way to the blackberries is no problem. The herd is quiet now and all bunched up to stay warm. I look for a familiar brown body in the field of Black Angus, but Awanita has not returned. Sue walks with me to the fence line. I rub her head and tell her to go back with the others and not to worry about me. I tell Sue that I am going to find her baby, and I tell her I am going to find my sister.

Just like Mom said, there is a narrow trail cut into the tree line. At the trailhead, I stop to look at the trees and the ground. I walk slowly and try not to think about being alone in the forest for the first time. My chest tightens, but I breathe through it. At the marker tree, I turn left, onto the Old Town Path. Bud was right. There is no need for blazes to mark the way. The forest floor is worn into an open channel as wide as Rattlesnake Creek. There is no way I can get lost. I start to run. Most of the trees, except for a few cedar and pine, have already lost their leaves. I can see the sky; I am not afraid.

I run until I might collapse. When I see a bluff shelter, close enough that I won't lose sight of the path, I stop and rest there. I climb up to the top of the bluff to look for Awanita or Dixie. There is no sign of either of them.

The Old Town Path stretches out in both directions for as far as I can see. I sit and listen. I have listened to the forest in my dreams and from Ayma's screen porch. But here on the bluff, the inside of forest sounds nothing like I expected. Somewhere, I know a barred owl is watching silently. What I hear in the afternoon light are trees. Not the wind blowing through them—I hear trees creaking back and forth to each other. All of them creak. At first, I am afraid the forest will fall. I lay my head on the rock and shut my eyes because the creaking makes me dizzy. The fall air on one cheek and the cool rock on the other remind me that I am in my forest, our forest. I am home, looking for Awanita and Dixie.

"Cricket?"

Dixie calls my name in the same raspy voice I've waited to hear since we were mocked on the bus. Whether I was defending our friendship or losing my mind when I made Delta bleed doesn't matter anymore. I am happy to hear Dixie say my name. I smile at Dixie, glad she has found me. Dixie sits down beside me, and we listen to the trees together. I take her hand in mine, and now the creaking of the trees sounds like a choir.

"We're sisters," I say.

"I figured." Dixie squeezes my hand.

I slide closer to Dixie and rest my head against her shoulder; we're sisters.

For the first time ever since I have known Dixie, I decide that I can be brave now, really brave, with her, not only for her. I stretch back on the rock, almost like when we were floating in the Sipsey, and Dixie stretches back, too. I take her hand to make a float-star, only we float ourselves in the sky instead of the river. There is a crescent moon hanging directly in the circle of empty tree canopy, waning toward nothingness.

"Dixie?"

She turns her face to mine.

"Delta added a knitting prayer for God to bring y'all a new mama."

Dixie looks away from me, and I keep holding on to her. I am sticking with Dixie.

"Dixie?"

She rolls over onto her side and grabs my face fully into her hands. "Cricket."

We listen to the trees until they're finished, and then I tell Dixie what happened with the cows and how Awanita is gone. Dixie listens to everything I say and nods. We are starting to lose sunlight; my new ease with the forest is shaky, especially as the sun goes down completely. I stand up to leave, and Dixie pulls me back down beside her.

"Wait," she says. "Just wait."

We sit for a few minutes longer, looking across the forest, down at the Old Town Path. I look toward Ayma's. The air is too cold for me, and soon I won't be able to see the sky.

The oldest trees here must be more than three hundred years old, set too deep in the ravine to have been timbered in the 1800s or even the 1990s. The young ones, the youngest that I can see with so little light, might be two or three. There are dead trees, leaning onto each other for support and slowly returning to the forest. And there are shadows among them—shadows that dance, shadows that run, shadows that urge me to go deeper.

I remember what Bud told me on the day we lost

Sue's calf. He told me that sometimes when we let go, that's when grace takes over. I decide to let go. I pretend the night is September and the air is warm. I let go of needing the blue sky, and I see the golden pink sky that is bringing the night. I don't need blazes to find my way.

Awanita stands there in the Old Town Path, looking up toward the bluff. He reaches his neck out to us and holds one leg high off the ground, like he might come closer. But just like in my dream, he doesn't linger; he has come to say good-bye.

"What do you see?" Dixie asks.

I shake my head.

Awanita is gone, spirited away into those shadows. Or perhaps he remains there watching us.

Dixie places her hand on my heart and takes my hand to her heart.

Looking at my sister, I do see her now almost exactly the same way she comes to me in my dreams. I am here, Dixie is here, and everything she ever showed me is right here above and below and around and inside me. Dixie bows her head for a long time. With Dixie's hand still on my heart, I ask grace to take over.

Chapter Thirty-six

FOR THIS WEEK, we moved the knitting circle up to tonight, election night, so all of us knitters can be here when Bud officially wraps up the campaign. We all want to be together when we hear the outcome. Ayma and the knitters all voted early. Louisa voted absentee because she's still recovering. Mom didn't move back in time to vote this year.

Now there is nothing to do but knit and wait. Since the campaign is over, we won't be knitting *Hale Yes!* scarves anymore. Hopefully, Bud will win tonight and we won't have to knit those for another three years. We've already started knitting shawls for the nursing-home residents. Truthfully, the more advanced knitters are working on ponchos for the nursing home, not shawls. That particular poncho pattern, with its scalloped edging, is still too complicated for me and a couple others, namely Mom and Delta.

We three knit our own projects. Mom and Delta have already started on their shawls. A shawl is really the same thing as a scarf only with double the stitches across. Then you add the pompons and it looks extra special.

Dixie is here with us, too. She doesn't knit. She writes stories and poems, mostly about Secret and Riddle. I know, because when Dixie writes one that especially pleases her, she gets me to read it out loud to the group. The knitters love Dixie's stories.

The special services lady from the county is the one who started Dixie writing. I've started to see this same special services lady, a psychologist, and I will see her twice a week. Her name is Rose Sheffield. She graduated high school the same year as Mom and Bud did. I didn't think I'd like her, but she's cool. She lets me call her Rose.

Rose says she is a lot like me. In fact, Rose herself can do six pull-ups, which is none too shabby for a grown-up. Rose is going to add a pull-up bar in her office door for me to use if I need to while I'm in there talking to her on Mondays and Wednesdays.

Mom added a real pull-up bar in my bedroom doorway, too. I don't have to use the closet bar anymore. She says she might use it one of these days. I suspect that won't be anytime soon because she is so busy dating Bud. They like to shoot pool together over in Winston County.

Bud's not expected here until eight o'clock or so. We've gathered early to be a support to one another. Madilee says she wouldn't be surprised if Jim Beckett himself voted for Bud—that made everybody laugh. I guess our knitting circle is sort of like the campaign headquarters. We are drawing them in tonight. Mom is holding up fairly well for being around so many people.

The ladies from Evelyn's have brought some leftover Brunswick stew, which they ran as a lunch special today in honor of Bud. I am sick of Brunswick stew, because that's all Bud makes. They brought lemon squares, too, which are a big hit. Evelyn made those especially for an election night treat. Evelyn has been married four times already, so she's giving Mom a few tips on snagging Bud. Mom's doing a good job at not getting offended. Dr. Jeter stopped by briefly, but we're all his patients, so I think he got freaked out.

I wash my hands from the lemon squares, pick up my needles, and cast on my new prayers:

1. Thank you for giving me the best family I could ever have imagined and for making my best friend my sister.
2. Thank you for my amazing pectorals, biceps, triceps, shoulders, and breasts.
3. Please get Mom a job in the forest.
4. Thank you again for getting Mom and Bud back together.
5. Thank you for Rose Sheffield understanding that I need to keep myself strong.
6. Please help me get off to a better start when I go back to school.
7. Please get Delta some freaking implants or something, so he will stop flicking those teeth.
8. Thank you for my time with Awanita, and keep him safe. Could I please see him now and then?
9. Please keep Dixie getting better, but don't let her change too much.
10. Just for good measure, though I know all the votes are in, please let Bud win tonight.

When I'm finished adding my prayers, Dixie hands me a sheet of paper. She doesn't knit, but she does like to have her own dedicated prayers included.

1. Thank you for bringing Cricket to Wren.
2. Thank you for Bye deciding to come here and live on Wren Mountain.
3. Keep my brother sweet.
4. Let Bud win tonight.

When I read this, I can hardly believe that Dixie calls Bud *Bud,* too, though I sure am not going to be able to call him anything other than *Bud.* I let it slide and add four more stitches, with Dixie's prayers, to mine. Who knows what prayers Delta has cast on? He is working away on his shawl.

By the time Bud strolls in, the house is packed with supporters, all of them having just voted for Bud. We have the TV on in the den, though we'll hear the results directly from the precincts long before the late news from Decatur reports out. Decatur usually doesn't report on Lawrence County elections until the late news, and then it's easy to miss because our results only scroll across the bottom of the screen.

Mom jumps up to see Bud practically before he can get in the door. He grabs her by the belt loop and pulls her in to him; he doesn't kiss her. All us knitters, and visitors, don't even bother to hide the fact that we're staring at them. Bud whispers into Mom's ear, hiding his mouth right in her hair, I guess so all of us gawkers can't read his lips. Whatever he says, it must be good. Mom looks at Bud and swallows hard, and turning all red in the face, says, "Oh, is that right?" Then she sort of pushes him away. I add one more prayer: *Lord, please give me the patience I'm going to need for these two.*

Ayma doesn't get up from her post, but she gives Bud two thumbs up from her chair and calls to him, "We're real proud of you, Bud. What news do you bring from the precincts?"

Bud does that thing where he takes his cap off and starts rubbing his hair, like he's nervous to say anything out loud. "Well, we won the high school by fifty votes." He reports this great news as if he were telling us what the mailman left in the box. This is big, victory-shaping news; the high school is Mr. Beckett's home precinct.

Bud continues, "They've run into some trouble at our precinct. An election officer forgot to record the starting count on one of the machines or something. One of Beckett's monitors is over there arguing with the precinct chief about tampering."

By the looks of it, Bud is not concerned in the least by that news. He fixes himself a bowl of Brunswick stew, nods his approval of it to Evelyn, then flops down between Dixie and Delta.

The party is so loud that when the phone rings at

nine o'clock, we nearly miss the call. It's Jim Beckett trying to track down Bud. We all stop knitting and talking when Bud takes the phone. Someone turns off the TV so we can better hear Bud's end of the conversation. "Yes, sir. No, I understand. Thank you. Thank you, sir. You have a good evening, too."

This time, when Bud grabs Mom's belt loops, he bypasses all the whispering into her hair business and pulls her straight in for a kiss. Mr. Beckett has conceded the race. Dixie and Delta and I hold on to each other and scream as loud as we can. We won.

Everybody starts screaming, "Speech! Speech! Speech!"

"I'm no good at speeches, other than to offer thanks to every one of you in this room. I do have something on my mind. Something we've been keeping a secret for too long."

Then Bud looks right at Mom. Mom starts swallowing hard and turning red in the face again and all over her neck. Our living room goes dead quiet. Madilee grabs Ayma's hand, and I can see she is holding her breath.

"I want to introduce y'all to the new range manager of our forest. You all know her, we all love her, and I know she is going to really help us."

Bud holds his hand out to Mom, for her to come to

the front of the living room with him. Ayma nods for Mom to get up there. The chorus of "Hale Yes!" swallows her right up.

"Here's Tabythia Woods, everybody — our new community liaison to the national forest," Bud announces.

Mom stands there, with both her hands in Bud's hands, looking at him and then looking down, but not saying anything. Mom swallows so hard and looks so scared that the whole room together says, "AWWW."

I cannot believe that Mom didn't tell me.

With her bad aversion to people, I am not certain what to expect from Mom, now that she has the spotlight. She clears her throat and takes in another swallow of air. Then, just how she is so good at doing when it counts, she looks directly into the hearts of all of us. She's quiet for a second, and I know that she's calling on the Holy Spirit to help her out. And I know for a fact that it will.

Mom doesn't stutter or waver. She makes a fine speech. "Well, I'll tell you what. It is good to be home. Thank you all so much for welcoming my daughter, Cricket, and me back to Wren. Just like each of you, we will never get this forest or Wren Mountain out of our blood or our hearts. I'm honored, finally, to be formally associated with the Black Warrior Forest, and I look forward to working with each of you."

Mom starts to sit down, then she holds her finger up to say one more thing. "I also want to thank each of you for all your prayers over the years and tell you just how good it feels to be reunited with our family—my mother, Mary Nelson, and Mary Harold's father, Bud." Mom is overrun with splotches, but she is doing a good job at being a controversial woman without running away. "You all have really welcomed Cricket and me home. Thank you."

Ayma looks over at me and winks. I know we are both thinking the same thing: She did it. Mom finally named my father for everyone to hear. I can't help myself and I don't even try. I run over to Bud, but he gets to me first and every part of me that never missed my father falls into his arms, so glad that he is mine and so glad he is Bud. I am not a little child to be scooped up and held like a baby; he holds me anyway, and this time it is Bud who cries. He cries and laughs and I do, too. Dixie saves us from carrying on like babies all night. She piles onto Bud and me; Delta is right behind her. My mom—*our* mom now—is beaming out from her heart. She looks radiant like the moon did on that night when she was leaving and took that tiny slice of us back to Virginia; she has made us all whole again in Alabama.

Everybody on Wren Mountain is freaking out.

Soon the Wednesday knitters close in around Mom to congratulate her. I hear Madilee boss Mom, "Come here, Bye, and let me squeeze your neck."

I hope that after the election we'll still have the knitting circle. I can already see that the knitters have big plans for Mom and Bud. They are going to need a place to talk about all of this.

Ayma can't help it; she won't let go of Mom. Mom doesn't seem to mind; she is holding tight to Ayma and me both. Ayma starts leaking big tears; she is so happy that Mom has finally come home for good. Mom drops my hand and takes a second to look directly into Ayma's swimming pools. "See, Mother? I came back to you."

Delta wraps his entire self around my mom's legs; he is crying himself, like a true knitter. I look at Dixie; she smiles at me like a girl, like a true girl. Tomorrow, I will have to face Gil Traylor and Russell Cauliflower and everyone else at school. I'm not worried; I'm ready for anything.

CHAPTER THIRTY-SEVEN

TODAY'S MY FIRST DAY BACK at school since my second suspension of the year and it's the day of the fitness test in PE. Before I'm allowed back in class, Mom and I meet with our principal, Mrs. Montgomery. She is a nice enough lady, who graduated high school with Mom and Bud, though I don't know if that is helping me at all.

Mom is doing a pretty good job in here. She is swallowing awfully hard in between sentences, but she is sticking to it that I am not a bully who beats people up for no reason. Mom explains that Gil and Russell have been provoking me since the beginning of school. She tells Mrs. Montgomery how those boys harass Dixie, too, and that I've been protecting Dixie from them. Mom's trying to avoid having to explain why I lost it on Delta. The principal is kind, but she is not letting me off the hook.

"Mary Harold," she tells me, "you're a strong girl and that's wonderful; I don't want you to change. The world needs more strong women like your mother and your grandmother. But you're going to have to find a more productive outlet than beating people up."

"Yes, ma'am," I admit. "I know."

"Have you ever thought about sports?"

"No," I tell her, "I hate sports." Mrs. Montgomery looks appalled.

Mom kicks me. Not enough to hurt, just enough to get my attention. Then she shoots her eyes toward the bookcase in Mrs. Montgomery's office. The principal must like sports. Trophies, team photos, every sort of sports recognition for golf, tennis, and something with a stick are crammed into the bookcase.

"Well, that's too bad. Winston County has a girl on their middle school wrestling team. Coach Simms wants a girl on our team. Of course, athletes must keep their grades up and avoid disciplinary action."

I look directly at Mrs. Montgomery and give her a

sincere smile like Mom taught me. "Thanks. I have Coach Simms later; I'll ask him about it."

Secretly, I hoped I might miss the fitness test. I don't care so much anymore whether or not I can do more pull-ups than Gil. I have lost so much training time between tending to the farms and knitting Bud's scarves that I'm not as confident in my latissimus dorsi strength as I was before I got suspended. Everybody knows that the best training for increasing your pull-up repetitions is to practice pull-up reps. I have fallen way behind in my training.

While I feel physically fit and right strong, I know for sure that my strength is not as concentrated as it was at the beginning of the school year, when I was practicing my pull-ups regularly. My strength is more spread out through my entire body. I may not have the repetitions that I will surely need to come close to Gil.

In gym class, the boys and girls do their tests separately and at different stations. I volunteer to go first at the pull-up station to go on and get it over with. When I step up to the bar, Coach asks if I choose pull-ups or the flexed arm hang. I choose pull-ups. I don't have to be told to use an overhand grip; I understand the difference between pull-ups and chin-ups.

I grab the bar and hang, trying to find my breath

before starting. Russell and Gil move into my line of vision; they are watching me. In fact, all of my classmates watch. When a girl gets thrown off the bus and gets kicked out of school twice even before Christmas break, I guess her ferocity stock goes up among her peers.

As I hang, Coach says, "All right, Miss Woods. Let's see what you're made of. Go ahead." All I can think of is how right now, I am wishing that I had kept up my training or at least added a knitting prayer for pull-ups. I decide not to psych myself out.

I know I am strong; my work on the farm keeps me that way. I can do this just fine. I exhale long and with the inhale pull myself easily up to the bar, my chin well above the required height.

One, I think, *easy.*

Two, easy.

Three, easy.

Four, easy.

Five, so freakin' easy.

By my eighth pull-up, the class has closed up around me, which raises the heat and stifles my breathing air. I need more room. On the ninth I think, *Step back,* but don't want to waste oxygen by saying it aloud.

Ten. Not easy.

Eleven. Y'all, step back.

Twelve. Damn, step back.

Thirteen. Crap.

Fourteen. Please step back.

After fourteen reps, I hang and try to breathe. There is no air. I search for a picture of something cool and sweet in my mind—floating in the Sipsey River.

Fifteen. Easy. At fifteen, my classmates are pumped up on my behalf. Nobody is yelling "dyke," probably because they know I won't hesitate to take teeth out of skulls if pressed.

Sixteen. Easy, thank you, Lord. I think of Madilee with her rolled-down stockings telling me that Jesus makes the difference.

Seventeen. Hard. Seventeen. Come on, Jesus, make the difference.

After the seventeenth pull-up, I lower myself extra slow and hang from the bar again, thinking. I could find another. I could dig deep and find eighteen.

Eighteen. Where's the bar? Damn, where's the bar?

I drop to the mat with only seventeen pull-ups officially completed. I did it! I beat Gil's record! I walk to the water fountain, leaving Gil Traylor to defend his last year's title and to now go after my new record. I am the first girl ever to hold our school's pull-up record. A girl in Georgia holds the national pull-up record. With thirty-nine pull-ups to her credit, she is going to be tough to beat. Forty-one pull-ups—that's my goal for next year.

As I pass by Coach Simms on the way to change out, he says over his shoulder, "Come see me about the wrestling team."

I am thinking, no way am I going to wrestle for him. First of all, Gil Traylor is on that team, and so is Cauliflower Boy; that would suck out loud. Second, Sue is probably bred back from the new bull and she might need me. Third of all, Mom just got to Wren; she might need me. What if the forest loses a big tree, like Sophia? Mom is going to need a support system. Fourth, I'm considering the idea of really truly taking Delta on as a little brother; if he were to do more work around the farm, then he would be less of a brat. That's my thinking, anyway.

I decide to go see Coach Simms just to check him off my list, so no one can say I was uncooperative.

"Here's my predicament, Miss Woods, and I sincerely hope you will help me out, because then I will be able to help you out. Jimmy Braddock, that's Coach Braddock to you, has got a girl over there in Winston County. Big girl, but not all muscular like you. Probably not as strong, either. I hear you wrestle cattle up there on Wren Mountain that'd put a grown man to shame. Anyhoo—"

Coach tilts his chair onto the back two feet and rests himself against the cinder-block gym wall.

I can't stand it when people say "anyhoo," but I'm hearing him out.

"None of my boys will wrestle her. Plain old, no how, no way, ain't gon' do it. That's a problem for my team because we keep forfeiting matches to her. She's never lost a match to Lawrence County, and that's an embarrassment to me! I need you."

Coach cups the back of his head in his palms and fans his elbows wide. He looks at me, waiting for an answer. I wonder if he spent his childhood getting into trouble for tilting so far back in his chair. Probably so. I heard from Madilee that Coach has an addictive personality; I figure he's addicted to chair tilting, among other things. I should add a knitting prayer for Coach Simms, just like his aunt Madilee has done.

Coach Simms has yet to tell me just exactly how my helping him will also help me. I wait, without saying a word.

"You've had a tough first half of the year?"

I look at the ground and nod. I reckon he heard that from a bunch of people, my friend Madilee included.

"These boys on my team, they can be real jackasses,

I'm sure. Pardon my French. What do you need, Miss Woods?"

With no regret or hesitation, I make a deal. "I'll wrestle for you, and I'll beat Jimmy Braddock's big Winston-County girl every time if you will get your boys to treat Dixie Hale and myself with decency and respect. In fact, they should be treating all the girls in this school with respect. You know, no name calling, no oogling, looking up dresses, no touching and rubbing, none of that stuff that makes a girl feel ashamed of herself. And they shouldn't call people retarded, especially not my brother. Can you make them change?"

I cock my head left and to make my point extra strong, I squint my left eye tight so it's obvious that I'm, you know, eyeballing him. I say to myself, *All right, Holy Spirit, do your work.* Then I tilt my own chair backward, but there's no wall there to catch me, so after just a second I set myself back down.

"Child, the apple hasn't left the orchard, has it? You sound like every Woods woman I've ever known."

I steal that sharp, little, quick-nod move from Delta. Coach Simms has given me a nice compliment, but he hasn't given me much confidence that he can deliver what I've asked. I remain silent, waiting for an answer.

"Big girl, fighting for the underdog!" Coach Simms laughs, and when he does, his chair slips a little.

I still don't seal the deal. I am sticking to my principle of waiting, and I know how this works. This is Holy Spirit Time. I wait for Coach to settle down and realize he's going to be the one to come to me.

He caves. "Change is a slow process, as you know. But it can be done. I've known all these boys since before they was born; they look up to me. I know their families, same as I know your family."

Coach holds his hand out to me. "I believe we've come to an agreement. Practice starts next week. Meantime, keep wrestling those steers, young lady."

He drops his chair back onto all fours and jumps up to shake my hand. I press Coach Simms' hand, like I mean business, the same way Bud did all during the campaign. All I had to do was ask.

I run to catch Dixie in between classes. Over the sound of lockers slamming in the hall, my classmates walk by, shouting, "Good job!" "Yeah!" I don't know if my new record held up or if they have just found a way to like me. It doesn't matter, because everybody won something important today. I smile and lean against my locker, hoping to hear just one more word.

I know what waits beyond these cinder-block walls,

and I am ready. When the last bell rings, and everyone else has gone, I hear what I need to hear.

"Cricket!" Dixie stands right beside me.

Now it's time. I link my arm with Dixie's. I'm going to ask my friend, my sister, to show me the deepest places of wild forest. Beyond the parking lot, beyond the blazes, and even beyond the Old Town Path, the Black Warrior is calling us.

ACKNOWLEDGMENTS

Even though my portrayal of Wren, Alabama, is imaginary, Wren is a special to me because of my grammy's stories, because of the Sipsey Wilderness, and because the cerulean warbler — a tiny pale blue bird struggling to survive because old-growth forests are struggling to survive — returns to the area for breeding every year.

Thank you to Martha Ann Terry and Marynell Burnett for sharing the history of Lawrence County. Thank you, Janice Barrett of Wild South, for helping me plan hikes into the Bankhead. I thank Robin Sabino of Auburn University's Echota Tsalagi Language Revitalization Project for your assistance with the word *awanita*. Bubba, Billy, and most especially my father-in-law, El Chiefo, thank you for letting me work cows with you. Thank you my knitting sprites, Emily and Madre, for your friendship and your patience with my sorry knitting skills ("stitch and bitch"). Thank you to Gail Bird Necklace for your blessing, Cherokee history insight, the drawing of our girl, and for just being you.

Thank you, my David Ethridge, for reminding me that books don't have to be perfect, but they do have to be finished. Mary and Glen, thanks for our deliberation and final consensus reached at Paradise Point that one good old moon is better than say, sixteen moons. Thank you, my family of readers: Judith Amateau, Leigh Amateau, Gail Bird

Necklace, Marynell Burnett, Penelope Carrington, David Ethridge, Mary Ellis Gregg, Ed Hall, Mary Kiger, Meg Medina, Maggie Menard, Nylce Prada Myers, Bubba Sanderson, Jan Tarasovic, Anne Westrick, and Erika Yssel.

Thank you to Candlewick Press commission reps, whose incredible work begins long before a book is released. I am especially grateful for the talents of copyeditor Hannah Mahoney. Sherry Fatla and Caroline Lawrence — I tell you what, y'all make some beautiful books. Nicole Raymond, thank you for making it so much fun to write this book and for your genuine kindness. Props to my agent, Leigh Feldman (Darhansoff, Verrill, Feldman Literary Agency) — my favorite person in all of New York City. Judy B., of Key West, thank you for reminding me to "Get that censor off your shoulder!"

My Karen Lotz, thank you for seeing the soul of this book before I did. Um, and, thanks for showing me.

Judith and Bubba — well, I guess I thank you most of all. I love you, and it is a wonderful thing to live right where I belong, with you two.